Fire Summer

Fire Summer

a novel

THUY DA LAM

Red Hen Press | *Pasadena, CA*

Book design by Mark E. Cull

Library of Congress Cataloging-in-Publication Data

Names: Lam, Thuy Da, 1971– author.
Title: Fire summer : a novel / Thuy Da Lam.
Description: First edition. | Pasadena, CA : Red Hen Press, [2019]
Identifiers: LCCN 2019017794 (print) | LCCN 2019021213 (ebook) |
    ISBN 9781597094641 (pbk) | ISBN 9781597098380 (e-book)
Classification: LCC PS3612.A543287 F57 2019 (print) | LCC PS3612.
    A543287 (ebook) | DDC 813/.6—dc23
LC record available at https://lccn.loc.gov/2019017794
LC ebook record available at https://lccn.loc.gov/2019021213

The National Endowment for the Arts, the Los Angeles County Arts Commission, the Ahmanson Foundation, the Dwight Stuart Youth Fund, the
Max Factor Family Foundation, the Pasadena Tournament of Roses Foundation, the Pasadena Arts & Culture Commission and the City of Pasadena
Cultural Affairs Division, the City of Los Angeles Department of Cultural
Affairs, the Audrey & Sydney Irmas Charitable Foundation, the Kinder
Morgan Foundation, the Meta & George Rosenberg Foundation, the Al-
lergan Foundation, the Riordan Foundation, Amazon Literary Partnership,
and the Mara W. Breech Foundation partially support Red Hen Press.

First Edition
Published by Red Hen Press
www.redhen.org

for ba má

We die with the dying:
See, they depart, and we go with them.
We are born with the dead:
See, they return, and bring us with them.
　　　　　　　　　　—T.S. Eliot

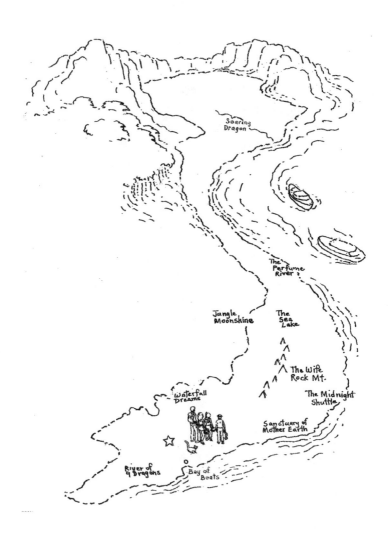

Soaring
Dragon

The
Perfume
River :

Jungle
Moonshine

The
Sea
Lake

The Wife
Rock Mt.

Waterfall
Dreams

The Midnight
Shuttle

Sanctuary of
Mother Earth

River of
9 Dragons

Bay of
Boats

Prologue

SHE WAS FREE at last. She gripped the railing of the now-abandoned fishing boat, its plank deck heaving beneath her feet. In the noon light, the distant island seemed to bob like a mossy green canteen on its side.

The captain and navigator, an old fisherman from a southeastern seaport of Vietnam they had escaped from a week before, had plunged in first. Others followed. The shoal of their black heads dipped and rose in the waves as the pouches and satchels strapped to their gaunt, sunburnt backs dispersed. A flock of seagulls circled and settled upon the crests to pick at the feast afloat on the South China Sea.

The woman looped the straps of her red shopping basket around her shoulder. She was glad her few possessions were in tightly sealed jars and plastic bags. When she hoisted her leg onto the railing, she noticed someone had scratched the date on the wood. *Bidon 18-12-1980.* She slowly raised herself and pulled up her other leg. She crouched there, feeling the pitch and wallow of the boat. As her body moved, she balanced herself and stood up.

White sand encircled the hilly island like a strand of luminous odd-shaped pearls. Farther inland, thatched roofs nestled beneath coconut palms that bowed toward the sea. She breathed in deeply, clasped her hands, and gazed into the water. She felt suddenly light.

She dove into a reflected sky.

As she submerged, the woman arched her back and lifted her head skyward to surface but slipped back instead. The ocean coursed through her body and pulled her down. The murmur of the sea lullabied her. She relaxed her grip, and the straps of her basket rose from her shoulder, scattering pictures of a husband on a bridge that hung across a river like a crescent moon and a daughter named after a blossom of the Lunar New Year. The ocean tugged at the woman's fingers and spread her arms. She soared through the clear blue sky.

One

Pearl of the Orient

WHILE SAIGON SLEPT at noon, Maia Trieu returned with her father's ashes. Her flight on the Boeing 707 from Los Angeles with a layover in Bangkok bore citizens of free nations. As she deplaned and bussed across the tarmac of Tan Son Nhat International Airport, she was caught in the intertwinement of yellow rice paddies and abandoned bunkered hangars, fusing in the summer heat of 1991.

Across the aisle, a man murmured about the humidity and wiped the sweat from his face with the back of his hand. When he pushed his dark hair off his forehead, she saw gray-green eyes, and her hand reflexively reached for the jade locket around her neck. The jade's muted color did not spark like the man's eyes, but the locket felt large and important on her. She gazed out at the midday mirage. Sunrays flickered on the hot asphalt runways and glimmered off wet rice paddies. Thirteen years earlier, she had escaped the country with her father, crossing the South China Sea in an overcrowded fishing boat to find asylum in America. Her hand clasped the octangular jade locket. *Ba, we're home.*

"That's a shame," the man said, looking past her through the window at the bunkered hangars. "A terrible shame." He peered through his camera and snapped several pictures. Besides a few Asian businessmen, the visitors were mostly Europeans, some from the newly unified Germany. The gray-eyed man of mixed ancestry was traveling alone. He looked at her. "Viet kieu?" he asked. His voice had a distinct American intonation. Except for a lightning bolt tattoo on his upper left arm, he fit the profile of an innocuous tourist. Beneath his relaxed exterior, she detected something else.

The trolley stopped at the terminal, and attendants in light azure áo dài pulled the glass doors open, greeting the visitors with the words of the yellow and red banner fluttering above. *Welcome to the City of Enlightenment!*

Rainclouds massed from the distant Western Range and lingered for the anticipated afternoon storm. The visitors left the stifling heat and entered the air-conditioned terminal.

"I'm JP Boyden," the man introduced himself and smiled. "And you are . . . *Pearl* . . . of the Orient?

"Maia Trieu," she offered her name matter-of-factly.

"Trieu? The maiden warrior from the third century A.D.?"

She shook her head, but he was already swinging a long imaginary sword and reciting lines from the legend of Bà Triệu in a resonant bell-like tone on riding the storm, slaying the behemoth, and rescuing the drowning in the Eastern Sea.[1]

Just then two oversize backpackers jostled past and knocked her off balance. JP Boyden grabbed her by the waist to keep her steady and held her close as the herd of travelers rushed by. "Why hurry?" he whispered. "Fast or slow, the checkpoints will be waiting." She pulled away and pushed through the crowd, but not before seeing a glint in his eyes.

At the checkpoint, she placed her shoulder bag onto the rolling metal bars before an x-ray tunnel. In Bangkok, the Thai officials had stepped back when they realized the cylindrical tin held ashes. Palms clasped, they had nodded her through. Now the Vietnamese stared at the black-and-white TV screen, speaking to one another in a northern staccato, too quick for her to understand.

What did they see? Could they see inside?

Bone white particles like sea coral and gray sand, ashes of a southern soldier escaped after the fall of Saigon, a daughter in his arms, now he in hers.

The muffled exchange stopped, and the men signaled her to step aside.

JP Boyden followed her. "How's your Vietnamese?"

She read aloud the VIỆT KIỀU sign that hung above the checkpoint and then switched to English. "Foreigners, the line is on the other side."

"You know," he said, "I'm looking for an interpreter."

She saw a bureaucrat in a crisp olive-green uniform approaching. Quickly assessing the American beside her, she asked, "Can you hold this?" as she passed the handbag to him. She placed a hand on his arm as if to keep her balance and bent down to fuss with the strap of her sandal.

"I'm here to write a travel feature," JP Boyden said, gripping her bag awkwardly, "and I need a local translator. You see, I've studied Viet at UH Mānoa, but it's still very basic. Chao co. Co dep lam! Bao nhieu tien?" He grinned with boyish satisfaction. "And I can count to ten: mot, hai, ba, bon, nam, sau, bay, tam—"

The customs agent interrupted him at eight. "Mời cô đi theo tôi!"

She stood up, a hand still on JP Boyden. "I can translate for you." Turning to the Vietnamese, she asked in a soft Saigon lilt, "Hàng này cho người ngoại quốc, phải không anh?"

The Vietnamese gripped her arm and ordered her to follow.

"What does he want?" JP looked at the official. "I'm an American journalist." He pulled out a glossy June 1991 issue of *USA News* and waved it in the official's face, on its cover— Sex, Lies, and Politics.

"You, American!" The official jabbed his bony index finger into JP's chest. "You go customs table."

"Where is he taking you?" JP turned to her, the handbag now dangling from his shoulder.

The official led her toward the glass doors at the far end of the terminal.

Her reflection belied what she felt inside. Dark eyes, a plain moon face, and straight hair gave her a child's mien. The white schoolgirl blouse and loose violet pants made her appear as fragile and benign as a morning glory.

When the door closed, the official released his grip and pushed her along the narrow corridor lit by dim florescent light. They turned corners and ascended steps. They passed closed doors spaced ten feet apart. The silence and stale air reminded her of the carpet hallway she had followed to the viewing room in South Philly five years earlier.

She had cried then and avoided her father's impassive face, staring instead at the bare cardboard casket. *Chết là sướng*, her father had said, his way of throwing up his hands, greeting life and death, his advice to his eighteen-year-old daughter to live bravely. *Your father fought with courage against the Communists.* The expatriates' homage rang in her ears. *For his service and sacrifice, he will be remembered.* In that last hour, before his body became ashes, bravery dripped from her eyes, each teardrop her inner voice calling across the border to the dead.

She was left at an open door.

The room had a wall mirror and a high window, through which sunlight cast a shadow on the man at the desk. "Sit down," he said, a faint northern accent. Brown sinewy hands opened a manila folder. "Triệu Hoàng Mai," he read her full name, reverting it to its native tones and order, "like the yellow flower that blooms on Lunar New Year in the South." He leaned forward, a compact man with intense eyes. "Twenty-three years old."

"Yes." She eased back into her chair. "Yes." She confirmed his next statement. "I was born on the Central Highlands in 1968."

"You left Vietnam with your father. Why did you leave?"

"I was ten years old."

"Who is your father?"

"He passed away."

"His rank in the U.S. puppet army?"

"He was a second lieutenant."

"Your mother's occupation?"

"We lost contact."

"What is the purpose of your visit to Vietnam?"

"I'm here to research Hòn Vọng Phu."

"Who's your sponsor?"

"The Museum of Folklore & Rocks."

"Will you be visiting relatives?"

"I hope to see my maternal grandmother."

"What do you know about anti-Vietnam groups—the GFVN, the FVO, the IVC?"

"I've never heard of them."

"On Tết this year, an overseas Vietnamese male was caught trying to return with terroristic intentions. To protect our country's independence, social order, safety, and territorial integrity, he was executed. What do you know about Huỳnh văn Vinh, a.k.a. Vinnie Huynh?"

"I don't know him."

The interrogator paused and sat back in the shadow. He asked about Little Saigon, Orange County. "Tell me about your daily activities there. Why did overseas Vietnamese in California vote Reagan-Bush and now Bush-Quayle? Explain your view on the recent fall of the Berlin Wall. What's your relationship with Jon Pōki'i Boyden? And who's the man in US Army fatigues in the picture he carries?"

JP Boyden had her bag when she left the interrogation. Along with a few selected visitors, they were herded onto an old Russian bus, whose black Cyrillic script remained visible under fresh layers of yellow paint. The bus left the airport for their temporary accommodation in downtown Saigon until their travel papers were cleared. After the midday sleep, the streets overflowed with people on bicycles, Vespa scooters, and three-wheeled xích lô.

"What's your relationship with Jon Pōki'i Boyden?" she mimicked the interrogator.

"You should have said something."

"Of course, I should have said something. What should I have said?"

"I'm writing a travel article on post-war Vietnam, and you're accompanying me as my interpreter. That's our story." The bus passed an ancient redbrick pagoda with a bell tower and twin pillars. JP released the cap of his camera, peered through the lens, and snapped several pictures of glassshard dragons in flight.

"What's the story with the strawberry?" She studied the insignia-like tattoo on his upper left arm.

She wanted to ask about the photograph of the GI in his wallet that the interrogator also questioned her about, but JP leaned over and whispered, "Our tour guide is watching."

The tour guide in the front seat next to the driver was her interrogator, who shifted his focus to the traffic when she caught his eye.

"Xuan is a People's Army veteran who knows the terrain," JP said. "Interesting fellow. He clearly believes that you're my girlfriend."

"I'm *not* your girlfriend. I *don't* need a tour guide in my country. *This is my country*." She lowered her voice. "I'm here on research—"

"To collect oral folk stories on . . ." He pulled out an embossed leather notebook, flipped through several pages, and read, "hon vong phu." He looked at her. "What's that?"

"How do you know this?"

"Customs personnel suspected that you might be a member of an insurgency. Are you?"

She flashed him a look that said his presence was unbearable.

"How about this for a headline? *Young Woman Returns to Continue the Work for Freedom*." He scribbled in his journal, in which he had already drawn lines and intersections and landmarks with fanciful made-up names, mapping their route in detail from Tan Son Nhat International Airport to downtown Saigon. "It's a justifiable story, isn't it?"

The bus stopped at the Hilton Inn near the junction where an urban canal emptied into the Saigon River. When they disembarked, she saw JP's deep frown. She quickly averted her gaze and squeezed in between a portly Frenchwoman and her stalky grandson.

The visitors tried to forget the annoyance of their delayed itineraries as they trailed Xuan through the common area on the ground floor. He informed them that the three-story inn was government-run and explained the list of rules for housekeeping, washing, and ironing. They had a six o'clock family-style dinner and a midnight curfew.

"It's bloody house arrest," a man grumbled.

Xuan stopped in front of an eight-by-ten framed picture of Vo Chi Cong on the wall. Next to the Chairman of the Socialist Republic of Vietnam was a life-size portrait of Ho Chi Minh in the garden of the Presidential Palace in Hanoi some thirty years before. To the visitors' amazement, Xuan read aloud the script beneath the portrait in near-perfect French—words copied from France's 1789 "Declaration of the Rights of Man and of the Citizen."

Les hommes naissent et demeurent libres et égaux en droits....
la liberté, la propriété, la sûreté, et la résistance à l'oppression.

"Maia," JP whispered, "how about you and me see the Pearl of the Orient tonight?"

"No."

They hauled their belongings up the circular stairwell and paused at the landing window, through which they could see the sky bulging with rainclouds. "The second floor is for the gentlemen," Xuan said, "the third, for the ladies."

"You have plans?" JP asked.

"I'm visiting my grandmother."

"Mind if I come along?"

Through the glass doors onto the veranda, the visitors watched the raindrops plummet into the Saigon River and flood the downtown streets where half-naked children splashed from puddle to puddle under the stormy sky.

Alone in the room, Maia sat on the bed and unzipped her bag. From beneath the travel kit of anti-malaria pills, iodine tablets, first-aid supplies, and a Swiss Army knife, she pulled out a bundle of clothes and unrolled it: a pair of black peasant pants, two light blouses, a pale yellow embroidered đồ bộ, and an old Dragonwell tin in which she carried her father's ashes, a bit of which she kept in her octangular jade locket. She put the tin on the rattan nightstand beside the bed. She caressed the yellow outfit, fingering the floral embroidery around the heart-shaped neck of the top and the silkiness of its matching bottoms. The bon voyage gift was as thin and velvety as rose petals, more like nightwear than street clothes, but the giver had assured her that she would blend in with the local womenfolk. She repacked and placed her bag at the foot of the bed.

She lay down, listening to the footsteps on bamboo flooring in the adjacent rooms and the pouring rain outside. She closed her eyes and saw satisfied gazes. She had not thought of returning until she stood in the headquarters of the Independent Vietnam Coalition in Orange County, California. She had stripped off her T-shirt and blue jeans, slipped on the delicate outfit, and then posed for scrutiny in the hall full of exiled Vietnamese. She saw longing in their eyes and heard anguish in their voices. She thought of her deceased father, and her desire for the home they had left more than a decade before surged through her. She believed she would be the one to return.

When she embraced the collective dream of the exiles, she felt she had made the right decision: to help the

Coalition contact her great-aunt, a former military commander the expatriates trusted was capable of instigating insurgency in the Central Highlands. Maia had not met her maternal grandmother's sister, but her face had been etched indelibly on her mind. From an old newspaper clip, Great-Aunt Tien gazed out—an open smile, wild long hair, and skin the color of her black clothes. Recently released from reeducation camp, E. Tien was the diasporic hope for a democratic government and repatriation. Whereabouts unknown. Locate her. Update her on the news from the Little Saigon headquarters and its alliance with those along the border of Vietnam and Cambodia. Contact made, Maia's mission would be complete.

A Glorious Return

WEST OF VIETNAM'S Central Highlands, somewhere between the Ratanakiri and Mondulkiri provinces, the early monsoon flooded the hilly terrain. Between the Sesan and Srepok rivers, red soil surged in streams, washing out the trails of men who now huddled in a thatched-roof makeshift on bamboo stilts. Through the breaks in the green canopy, they could glimpse the sky and imagine a glorious return.

"Eh, Vinnie!" Lee called from the hut. "Come eat." Lee stepped out on the veranda as rain sluiced off the peaked roof onto the flowing land. The aroma of charred kouprey and manioc diffused into the rain-soaked jungle. Lee removed his narrow-framed glasses and wiped the lenses on his peasant pajamas, a size too small and ill fit for his husky build. When he returned the glasses to his eyes, he peered again into the vaporous night.

Vinnie Huynh, outstretched on an old frayed hammock knotted from parachute nylon and strung from tree branches, chanted a bastardized "Katyusha" deliriously. The rain splashed on his pale ghostly face, drenched his ripped Levi's and Ranchero Stars and Stripes boots, tapped and bounced off the M-16 on his chest.

"Thằng ngu dại," Lee muttered and limped into the downpour in blackened US Army boots. Vinnie's naiveté reminded Lee of his own youth before the draft more than two decades ago. Dead of pneumonia before you make good with karma, Lee's old tūtū would have said. He made a futile effort to wring the cold rain from his overgrown hair.

Lee kept a hand on Vinnie's shoulder as they felt their way across the flooded campground. They stepped around bomb craters that overflowed like giant goblets of burgundy toasting the pouring sky. A Russian Minsk leaned against the crater's edge where Vinnie had crashed and bathed the morning of his arrival.

"Wait! My wheels." Vinnie broke free from his companion's grip and waded toward the motorcycle, tugging the M-16 through the red muddy water.

"Leave it. And return the rifle to the cave."

The men had never remained at one spot for long, but when they discovered a womb-like tunnel in the belly of the Annamite Range, they decided to camp there for the monsoon season. They buried the bones they found in the cave and made offerings, asking permission of the old dead to use the area as an ammunition depot. Outside the cave, they erected their shelters on bamboo stilts.

"Let me carry this," Vinnie said, clutching the rifle close to his chest. "I'll guard us against spies, VCs, wild beasts—" He stopped and then whispered, "Did you just see that?" He slowly aimed the M-16 at the shadow beyond the bamboo thicket. Before Lee could stop him, Vinnie squeezed the trigger.

The gunshots shattered the lulling pitter-patter of rain. Men bolted from the thatched hut with weapons in hand. Some fled to the ammunition depot while others dove into the jungle.

"Bravo! Bravo!" A pair of crippled hands clapped from the window where yellow lantern light illuminated the drizzling night. The paralyzed cook was the only one of twelve who did not participate in drills or emergencies. "Another kouprey?" Cook Cu asked. "Snakes, lizards, geckos—delicacies for my moonshine?"

A voice came from the cave. "What did he hit?"

"Nothing," answered a man in a bush.

"The kid's trigger-happy," concluded another behind a rock.

Near the bamboo thicket, they found Kai, a dark-skinned waif, who was foraging for wild berries and mushrooms. He seemed unrattled. The youngest of the group, Kai carried at his side a long machete he used to clear paths and mark trails through the dense jungle.

The men returned to the shelter. That was the second time Vinnie startled them. Just a week earlier, he roared unexpectedly into camp on the Minsk. His appearance and knowledge of their location made them uneasy, but they believed him when he said he was sent from America. He had come via Thailand, crossing at Poipet into Cambodia, driving eastward nonstop for two days. Now, he opened fire at the slightest shadow.

After the commotion, the men ate and drank heartily. A bottle of Jack Daniel's, packs of unfiltered Camels, and news from the Little Saigon headquarters lifted their spirits in welcoming the Year of the Goat. More than two decades in the jungle had blurred their military ranks, national allegiances, and vital statistics. Except for the bald ailing cook and young boy, the men's features—like those of Lee Hakaku Boyden's—were buried under shrouds of dark overgrown hair. Sometime during the Second Indochina War, the loose band of twelve had formed. They drifted back and forth across the border of Vietnam and Cambodia, ghostly vagabonds roaming a wasteland, not sure whether they were dead or alive.

"They sent a girl?" Cook Cu asked, his atrophied legs crossing stiffly on the kouprey hide. Before the rain, he had sprawled out on the mossy jungle floor beneath the burgeoning evergreens where the B-52s had failed to hit. "This is our home now," he had told Kai, pointing to a spot beneath a creaking pine where they could see the mountain ridge trailing the sky. "When the wind shakes the pine, the roots sway like the rocking of a sampan drifting on the Perfume River of the old imperial city." The paralyzed cook asked Kai to mark the gravesites beside the tilting pine.

"They're sending a girl," Vinnie said.

"Girls are good for *some* things."

The men chuckled and sipped their rice whiskey, reveling in the warmth that spread through their bodies. As the night fell, the rain pitter-pattered and the wind gushed through the cracks; they felt their isolation. They thought of their homes and the women from past lives and wondered what had happened.

Even young Kai looked momentarily lost. After a hamlet on the outskirts of the Central Highlands was burned to the ground, Lee had found a scorched child. He dropped the things he carried, tucked the dark waif into his cut-up duffel bag, and walked westward into the jungle of Cambodia. The child was named Kai for the cool peaceful sea that Lee remembered of his own home on a far-off island in the Pacific. More than any other member, Kai belonged to the wilderness, to the perpetual cycle of destruction and renewal, yet at times, his innocent eyes seemed to long for permanence, a place to call home.

"Who's the girl?"

"*A decoy,*" Vinnie said.

The jungle moonshine tasted grainy and bittersweet as he recalled how customs agents had interrogated him and stopped his physical entry at Tan Son Nhat International Airport, denying his return to the land of his origin.

The Other Side

THE WOMAN HITCHED the weight of the cripple up on her back. She moved slowly though he was only skin and bones. The straps of the red basket cut into her forearm, and the glass jars and bottles knocked against each other, sloshing water full of debris from the South China Sea.

I should throw them all away, she said to herself. *What does it matter now?*

His spirit seemed heavier than his ashes, which she had placed in a sealed jar before the failed escape. The nuns at Ox Pagoda had warned against crossing the ocean with human remains, but it was so her husband would have his kid brother with him. The woman continued down the sandy footpath with the spirit of her crippled brother-in-law on her back.

"Put me down," he wheezed again.

"And leave you in the middle of the road?"

"You could have left me on the back beach with those chess players. They would have given me a drink."

"Drink-drink-drink," she scolded him. "Chết là phải!"

"Death is contentment." His eyes closed halfway, his bony chin rode on her shoulder, and his shaved head bobbed as she plodded on. "I was contentedly dead before you brought me along in your jar."

"You wanted to see America."

"When I was alive!"

Her thin back curved under his weight, and his twisted feet dragged on the ground, but she kept treading as if they were still at sea. When the currents had returned her to the back beach of Vung Tau, she found her brother-in-law Hai washed ashore beside her. Without a word, she hoisted him onto her back, looped the handles of the basket of what remained around her arm, and trudged off over the sand where beachgoers lounged, oblivious under the sun.

"Steeped in moonshine, I was," Hai croaked. "Now an anchovy in brine, a cup of rice wine would be fine, oh fine."

"Have you seen a shuttle to Saigon?"

"Why don't you leave me here?" He lifted his head. "Look, over there."

In the distance, they could see a roadside café—a broken glass case of assorted cigarette cartons, beer cans, and Coca-Cola and Orange Cream bottles. A blue-and-yellow striped umbrella shaded a girl lazing in a hammock and two men sitting on low wooden stools.

The woman stopped to hike Hai up on her back. "Về nhà rồi tính."

"Home?" He chuckled dryly. "By now our house's been confiscated. You'd be thrown back in jail. No, no, no. A drink, I need a drink."

When they neared the café, their nostrils were stung by smoke, gasoline, and gunpowder, and their throats tightened. They realized the two men were teenagers in scorched peasant rags. Hai's knobby fingers dug into her collarbones. "Don't stop. Walk faster."

The woman lowered her head and moved as quickly as she could, the jars and bottles clinking loudly in her basket, water dripping.

"Set him down and rest," one of the boys called in a northern voice.

The woman glanced up and saw eyes squinting at her from a burned face.

"Nhìn thấy hãi cơ?" the boy asked. His mouth opened wide and eyes squeezed shut as if laughing. "You look creepy, too."

"Don't listen," Hai whispered. "You're just a little green and bloated."

She stopped before the two boys. "Does the bus to Saigon pass through here?"

"A jitney comes at nightfall," the burned face replied. "We're going to Ho Chi Minh City to catch the train north to be home for Tết."

"Is it Tết already?"

"Four more days 'til the Year of the Rooster," his friend said. He was missing a right arm and part of his upper torso.

"It's February 1981!" Hai croaked, calculating aloud the number of days that they had been at sea. "Twenty in December . . . thirty-one in January . . . Fifty-one. We've been gone for almost two months!"

"Let him rest against here," the boys said.

They lifted Hai off her back and propped him up amid a pile of dried coconut husks. The one with the hole in his chest lit a cigarette and tucked it between Hai's parched lips. The burned face dug two paper coins from his ragged pants pocket, held them up to his squint, and offered to buy them drinks.

"How far did you get?" the vendor asked. Her thick make-up did not mask her swollen pale skin but made her appear like a character from a cải lương folk opera.

"Bidon Isle," Hai said, his gnarled fingers clutching a Bia Saigon. "Everyone dove for it. My sister-in-law jumped in. People swam, swam, and swam." He stopped mid-story.

The xe lam arrived at nightfall, jam-packed with riders and tilting to one side from the unbalanced load on its roof. The three-wheeled jitney skidded to a stop, and the driver hobbled from the cab to the rear to shove the passengers further into the overcrowded compartment, forcing the mass of bodies to bulge through the side openings. He nudged the woman onto a stranger's lap while pulling at her basket, a momentary tug-of-war until she clasped the basket to her chest and he let go.

"Strap the cripple to the roof," he ordered.

Ignoring the driver, the two boys from the North stuffed Hai into the passengers' compartment, his bony limbs bending as he folded into the gaps between intertwined bodies. The boys wedged their feet onto the flimsy back step and clung onto the roof's edge. When the overloaded vehicle sputtered and then accelerated, the boy with one arm was blown off-balance, but he quickly steadied himself. The wind howled through the hole in his chest and filled the woman with emptiness as vast as the sea. The jitney careened through the night toward the lights of Ho Chi Minh City.

When the jitney stopped at the night market where peddlers lined the alleyway leading to her home, the woman smelled sundried anchovies, crispy fried Chinese crullers, and freshly baked French baguettes. There was something she had not noticed before—the earthen odor of oxen in the humid heat after the afternoon rain. She realized then why the neighborhood was called Ox Alley though they were long gone by the time her husband relocated her family from the Central Highlands to the southern capital one fiery summer.

The trail of pale lantern lights, flickering fireflies in the night, beckoned the northern boys to disembark. They untangled Hai from the ball of knotted bodies and insisted on carrying him home. The cripple, flanked by two teenagers to whom he promised the barrel of rice moonshine he had distilled, and the woman with the basket full of ocean debris, all merged into the market where people spoke an unrecognized language. When the woman strained her ears to listen, she caught distinct phrases she knew, interwoven with other familiar yet incomprehensible tongues. People moved side-by-side, crossing into each other's path, overlapping like a palimpsest. It occurred to her that now she could see her hairstylist friend. She told Hai and the boys to go ahead home.

At the entrance to Phoenix Salon, the woman called out to her friend, "Đẹp ghê ta!"

"Ghê là đúng," Phuong replied and lifted her long side-swept bangs to reveal a deep gash across her forehead. She rolled up a pants leg to expose another scar on her knee.

The woman said, "I should've taken my own advice and jumped off the train with you." She eased into a chair and leaned her head back into the basin.

"What's the story with you and the warden?" Phuong asked.

"I should've learned how to swim." The woman sighed, welcoming the cool water on her dry, itchy scalp. "Or at least brought a life jacket."

"Bồ kết shampoo?"

"Who would have thought? You bring pictures of your family, you bring gold leaves sewn in your hems, and you bring ashes—"

"Your brother-in-law Hai's ashes?"

"In an old jar of mắm cá lóc in this shopping basket." She laughed, remembering Hai's objection to the smell of fermented snakehead. "We were almost there."

"It's fate."

"Is it my fate to be married at sixteen? What would life have been if I were a young girl or an old woman when the North came south? But I was twenty-five. A husband and a daughter one day, and the next, they're halfway across the world. My happiest years were in prison. Did I tell you?"

"What's the story with you and the warden?" Phuong asked again.

"You just accept. Who would have thought? The currents didn't even take us to the other side."

Winter Night Café

As NIGHT FELL over Ho Chi Minh City, the neon pink sign glowed: WINTER NIGHT CAFÉ. The xích lô had left Maia and JP in front of the garden café, where white plastic chairs and round tables were strewn around a stage under a sprawling starfruit tree. A skeletal kitten slinked through the *Ochna integerrima* hedge. Its mouth opened mutely.

"Your grandmother lives *here*?" JP asked.

Maia checked the address on the envelope and looked for a street number on the entrance. The wooden gate was a familiar sight though freshly painted in a different color. The hoàng mai hedge in summer bloom with bright red sepals and dark glossy berries was as she remembered. On stage, a girl in black tights crooned "Unforgettable" as the patrons smoked and sipped on iced café au lait.

"Here, Pōpoki," JP called, and the scrawny orange stray tottered over. When he picked it up and scratched under its chin, it gazed at him fixedly with pale yellow eyes. "Look," JP said. "The little fella has a protruding belly button."

They entered the outdoor café, the kitten tottering behind. They sat at a peripheral table. The kitten clambered up onto JP's lap and curled into a spiny orange ball.

The girl in black tights came over and smiled broadly at JP. "Hi, Big Guy! My name is Na. Bia Saigon? Bia Hơi? Bia Ôm?"

When Na returned with a Saigon beer and càphê sữa đá, JP invited her to join them. Na plopped into the chair beside JP and immediately intrigued him with her stories.

Though her oblique black eyes, long wavy hair, and dark skin alluded to her mixed parentage, she did not speak of it.

Maia observed the waning gibbous moon through the starfruit tree and thought of her mission.

"Time to visit family and resolve whatever questions you might have." The Independent Vietnam Coalition had agreed.

"I just have my grandmother's last letter," she had said.

The address was the only shred of evidence that linked her to the past. A flimsy, inconsequential piece of information she was allowed to carry with her. It was an address of a maternal grandmother she barely knew, an address the Coalition had thought no longer existed.

"Whatever you do," the Coalition instructed, "be at the foot of the Vong Phu Mountain on the first night of the full moon."

A shooting star flashed across the sky. Maia heard faint laughter and was reminded of her childhood when she had climbed the tree with the neighborhood kids. They would squeeze onto the narrow plank wedged between the V-shaped trunk, scared and exhilarated at the height and closeness to the sweet, tangy starfruit.

"You know why no customers?" Na asked when it was time to close the café. Her mischievous eyes surveyed the dark surroundings. "This place is haunted—" She stopped and looked toward the man-dug fishpond. She whispered, "Someone is here." It could have been the different time zones, the mix of alcohol and caffeine, or Na's easy laughter. Whatever it was, the threesome peered intently at the approaching shadow. "It's coming!" Na let loose a string of shrill laughter. The kitten leaped from JP's lap, baring its fangs as if hissing at the shadow.

"Xuan!" JP exclaimed. "It's Xuan."

"We should go," Maia said. "It's almost curfew." She stood up, but JP had already risen, shaken hands with the tour guide, and pulled out a chair for him.

"Didn't think we'd bump into you here," JP said.

Na eyed Xuan. "You scared us."

Maia picked up the skeletal kitten by the nape of its neck like a sack of bones and gathered it on her lap. "Na thought you were a ghost."

"Nonsense," Xuan said.

"So brave!" Na said. "You'll be visited—"

"This place is haunted," JP mimicked her. He had given up on a serious conversation with Na. She had talked openly about being the café's singer-hostess, her likes and dislikes, and her dream of one day opening a café of her own. She had let him touch her smooth lineless palms and boasted their absence of fate's grooves. But when he said he was hapa with a lineage from the Middle Kingdom and asked if her father was American, her face changed.

"Big Al from Love City works in passport," she blurted out. She then clammed up and became cross. She preferred ghost stories, believed in the afterlife, and claimed to converse with spirits.

Maia shifted in her chair, aware of Xuan's eyes.

Na began an unsettling story that had been told around Ox Alley since the abandoned property was first expropriated. A young official had relocated his widowed mother from the North and turned the cactus orchard into a popular outdoor nightspot, which, for reasons only a few knew, he called Winter Night Café. Once in the airy house, they felt another presence. At night, they would hear a woman chanting. The official's elderly mother made repeated offerings and set up an altar shop next door, but the spirit would not leave. "The ghost," Na whispered. "Her husband built the house for her."

Maia's breath stopped. Fragments of people, places, and her father's stories surfaced. She remembered the two-story L-shaped house with a balcony overlooking her grandmother's orchard. In the summer of fire when the North pushed south and central Vietnam dissolved in flames, her father evacuated the family and in-laws from the highlands to Saigon. He built a home for his wife and daughter in a pocket of verdant land, an oasis in the concrete city, he had inherited with his crippled kid brother. His mother-in-law moved into the groundskeeper's cottage and cultivated purple dragon fruit.

The night air turned chilly in the outdoor café.

Maia heard JP's question. "How did the woman die?"

Leaning forward, Na's eyes narrowed. "No one knows." The dark clouds of hair hovering over her high forehead made her appear impishly grand, looking down on them and conjuring up their lives. A slow smile possessed her lips. "Lovesick maybe."

Xuan slammed his beer on the table. He fumbled in his pocket for a cigarette, lit it, and took a long drag. He settled into his chair, and for the rest of the night, he did not speak. They could not see that he was no longer watching them or that his eyes had softened. The beer toppled and rolled off the table onto the gravel, where the orange stray slinked over, sniffed, and lapped up the foamy liquid.

"What happened to the orchard keeper?" JP asked.

"Her younger daughter married the official," Na said. "And they all moved to the River of Nine Dragons."

Phat Salon

NO ONE HAD seen the dragon, only traces of its inky tail across the right collarbone of the owner of Phat Salon in Little Saigon, Orange County. The tail undulated as Phat cut a client's hair and styled a look that revealed the woman's true inner self.

"Inner-outer correlation," he would say.

The transformation began with Phat serving the client a cup of hot herbal brew and a slow, deep massage of her feet until she sighed softly. He would then leave the room. When he returned, he cut the woman's hair in a single fluid motion as she gazed at her reflection in the mirror and imagined the hidden dragon on his supple body—hairstylist by day and mixed martial artist by night.

Curiosity drew a steady stream of patrons to Phat Salon on Bolsa Avenue.

A flying dragon with enormous bat-like wings, a client whispered.

A sea dragon rises from the East, another said.

Phat's ex-girlfriend from Berkeley had the last word: a black serpent coils tightly around his hard torso and breathes fire on his sex.

But Maia knew the creature was incomplete. What Phat had was only the tip of a tail. When the tattoo needle hit a nerve on his shoulder blade, Phat's body went into shock. He fainted and was rushed to the emergency room.

Maia also knew it was not a dragon tail.

"A fish tail?" Phat repeated in disbelief, looking up at Maia from the low wooden stool, his fingers interlocking her toes. She was a walk-in, long straight hair dry and brittle with split ends from four years of college in the Northeast snow belt.

"A monstrous fish," she said and told him a fish story she had read in her folklore class. Though Phat was not convinced even after the day she showed him the enormous fishtail stone displayed at the Museum of Folklore & Rocks where she was the curator's new assistant, they quickly became friends.

In Little Saigon, where people consumed U.S. goods and participated in Vietnamese rituals and festivities, Phat and Maia, orphans at an early age, tended to the void of their parents' absences in different ways. Phat further emptied himself in order to flow and become ungraspable, a defense in the martial arts ring and in life. Maia filled her void with stories. Phat strived to be mirror-like; she sought mirrors.

When word arrived that Vinnie Huynh went missing after landing at Tan Son Nhat Airport on Tết, the Independent Vietnam Coalition approached Maia with an offer of a research grant, with one stipulation: she was to be the liaison between the Coalition and E. Tien. Maia could not refuse the opportunity to travel to places she had only studied and read about in library books. She convinced herself that accepting the assignment was an act of love for her late father—to continue his legacy. The return was a chance to reconnect with family.

A week before her trip to Vietnam, Maia made an appointment at the salon. Phat served her a cup of warm herbal tea and massaged her heels, arches, and toes. He meditated and meditated but could not see her true inner desires.

He finally asked, "You're returning to Vietnam to collect stories on *rocks*?"

"In four provinces, from central Vietnam to the northernmost border with China, stands a wife-rock atop a mountain cradling a child waiting for her husband's return. Some believe he's gone fishing in the South China Sea; others say he's gone off to war. The story of Hòn Vọng Phu, a wife who turns into stone waiting for her husband's return, shapes and is shaped by the physical terrains of Vietnam and the people's expressions."

He seemed unmoved.

She repeated the questions from her college project: "Why is Hòn Vọng Phu so prevalent in the imagination of the Vietnamese? How have the tale and its modern adaptations transformed in the diasporic community, where a confluence of histories, cultures, and languages interact? How do these stories narrate Vietnam's national identity?"

He gave her a blank stare.

She then showed him the news clip of E. Tien. "I've been tasked by the IVC to look for my great-aunt."

He remained silent.

She finally pulled out an old yellowing envelope with the address from her maternal grandmother's last letter and told him the real reason for her wish to return. "Someone there might be able to tell me what happened to my mother. Even if this were *all* a dream," she said, forestalling his butterfly dream parable, "I'd still want to know."

He trimmed her split ends but left her long hair as it was, a drying river seeking the sea.

Eyeball

WHEN XUAN VEERED the red Honda Dream off National Highway 1 onto a dirt trail that led into an old rubber plantation, Maia's first thought was to hop off the backseat, dash for the main drag, and hitchhike to catch up with Na and JP. In her mind's eye, she could see Na's hair blowing like rainclouds, JP hanging onto the motorcycle's rear grab bar for dear life, and No-No Pōpoki curling into a spiny orange ball in the front basket. Traveling on two motorcycles 136 kilometers southwest of Ho Chi Minh City over hills and valleys and through farmers' markets and rice paddies, they would arrive in the Mekong Delta before nightfall. That morning, Na had sped off with JP on the used Minsk he had bargained down to 250 USD, leaving Xuan and Maia to follow. They were all going to the River of Nine Dragons to look for Maia's maternal grandmother. But now Xuan left the highway and lost Na and JP.

The dirt trail cut through the rubber forest, a colonial past buried deep in the red soil. The hum of the motorcycle's engine momentarily halted the shadows of workers tapping the trees to drain their milky liquid into aluminum buckets. Beyond the old plantation, the trail widened and curved along muddy ponds of ivory lotuses. The motorcycle's wheels skidded over the swampy ground, and the stench of algae rose with the morning sun. From time to time they would pass a roadside eatery, its menu painted white on the tree bark, inviting passersby to stop for *Hủ Tiếu Nam Vang, Dừa Tươi & Bia Hơi*.

The path gradually wound upward to an empty lookout at the foot of the mountain. A barefoot boy about seven or eight loitered nearby, hawking still life drawings of five fruits that looked like naked ladies. "Mâm ngũ quả!" he cried. "Mâm ngũ quả!" He had a three-patch hairstyle of the late sixteenth century and a cheeky singsong voice.

> *The lady's head is a pomelo,*
> *her eyes like longans,*
> *breasts like peaches,*
> *palms like Buddha's-hands,*
> *her garden, a fragrant wedge of jackfruit.*[2]

Xuan ignored the boy and his portrait of a naked lady and parked the motorcycle next to the motley tents along the mountainside. The makeshifts fluttered in the breeze, but not a sound or movement came from inside. At the far end of the tents sat an enormous water-damaged wooden crate, silent and still like the mountain. Xuan walked to the crate and examined its faded print. BANGALANG 5-26-1830. He peered through the cracks into the pitch-dark interior. He kicked it. The sodden wood gave a long, hollow creak.

Beside the crate, Maia leaned on what she had first thought was a sun-warmed boulder. She was startled when she realized it was the rounded back of an old sleeping camel. She had never been up close to a great beast of burden. She gingerly caressed its graying head and stroked the tough leathery skin of its cheek. Its outstretched neck sank farther onto the ground. Its large eyes squeezed tight, shutting out the midday light. She did not question the camel's presence at the foot of the mountain but found comfort in the steady rise and fall of its heavy, laborious breathing.

Xuan paid the fruit boy one thousand đồng to watch the motorbike and motioned Maia to follow. As they climbed the stones that were leveled in the slope, she silently rehearsed the reasons for her return. She chanted a mantra she had learned from a laminate pocket-sized picture of Quan Âm: "Nam mô A-di-đà Phật. Nam mô A-di-đà Phật. Nam mô A-di-đà Phật." She cleared her mind in anticipation of what was to come. When she looked up, she saw a looming French cathedral with twin steeples. The red tile pitched roof with upswept eaves reminded her of a Chinese pagoda. The high tower's eastern and western arches and angles fused seamlessly with the natural folds of the mountainside, shrouded in low-hanging clouds.

On the summit, three men in green public security uniforms were playing cards at a stone table under a flamboyant tree. They left the game as soon as they saw Xuan and Maia. The men's sandals dragged over the ground and disturbed the red dirt that rose in a haze and fell on their gnarled toes. The smallest marched with heavy steps toward them as if weighted down by a great burden. "You've come on time," he said, his accent from the northern countryside.

Xuan nodded at the small man, whom he called "Comrade Ty," and acknowledged the other two at his heels. Pâté was stocky with a plump liverwurst face. Cross-eyed Lai had pale translucent skin that stretched over his stick frame. "They want to ask a few questions," Xuan said.

A gust of wind blew a cloud of scarlet blossoms off the flamboyant branches. The blossoms fluttered and ascended like butterflies before falling. Beyond the front yard, the land dropped off steeply into rice terraces that bejeweled the earth with emerald and gold.

"Awfully pretty," fat Pâté murmured. He took her hand and pulled her to the stone table. His chubby thumb stroked the top of her hand, his eyes on her jade locket. He suddenly reached over and yanked the locket from her neck. The chain broke and slipped to the ground. The jade was in his fleshy palm.

"What's inside?" he whispered. His knees started to bounce.

"My father's ashes."

"Sister," the leader said, "you've returned for what purpose?"

The locket was passed from Pâté's clumsy fingers to Cross-eyed Lai, who tried to pry it open with his long pinky nail. "Đéo mẹ!" Cross-eyed cursed when his nail snapped. He pulled out a pocket-sized stiletto and wedged its sharp tip into the octangular jade case.

"I'm collecting stories on Hòn Vọng Phu."

Pâté's legs stopped bouncing. "Hòn Vọng Phu? The trilogy Hòn Vọng Phu 1, 2, and 3—'The Army Departs,' 'Eternal Waiting,' and 'The Husband Returns'?" His patchy moon face beamed at her. "We're the Public Security Trio, third place in last year's Mekong Songfest. Comrade Ty is our lead man!" He pounded a marching rhythm on the stone table with his fists, and in a deep baritone, he sang the first "Hòn Vọng Phu," in which soldiers depart for war. Cross-eyed Lai dropped the jade locket into his back pants pocket and joined in with a high-pitched voice, his bony fingers intricately picking the strings of an air guitar.

"Pâté! Lai!" The leader shushed them after the first verse.

"Curtains?" Pâté asked in a small squeak. He turned to her and said, "Sister, you don't listen. We'll all be drenched."

Pâté and Lai disappeared into the temple and returned with two red curtains. They tore the curtains lengthwise into strips and then braided and knotted the strips into a thick long cord. With a quick movement, Lai twisted Maia's arms behind her, and Pâté tied them with a red band. They roped her ankles.

Pâté and Lai walked to a giant blue globe perched on a pedestal beneath the gutter of the temple roof. On the side of the globe, a painted long leaf-shaped eye stared out amidst white clouds. The top had been broken to catch rain.

The men tossed one end of the cord over an upswept eave about ten feet above. It hooked on the eave and dangled four feet from the ground. The other end lay slack.

The leader kneeled down, and with surprising strength, he scooped her over his shoulder and carried her to the globe. They tied her bound ankles to the slack end of the rope. The leader pulled the other end and hoisted her off the ground. Pâté and Lai pushed the giant eyeball beneath her.

Her world was inverted.

Blood rushed to her head as her body dangled over the sphere's jagged edges. She smelled salt. She straightened her posture like a soldier marching off to war, but she was in black peasant pants and tied upside down with red ropes. When she looked into the sphere, she saw petals drifting like dismembered butterflies. She thought of her father and his fight. Her head became heavy and hot as blood pulsated faster and faster toward the steady hum of whirling blades chopping air.

Thwack. Thwack. Thwack.

Her father commanded the pilot to lift off from the burning land. Her mother curled around her, covering her from the scorched bodies and homes ablaze. Her grandmother and aunt huddled beside them. As the Huey maneuvered southward for Saigon, the summer of fire ignited a flame in her young heart.

"We don't need to do this," the leader said.

The first time they dunked her, she squeezed her eyes shut. When they raised her, the leader's face was inches from hers.

"Who sent you? Why have you returned?"

The intervals in the water became longer. Each time she was hauled up, her interrogator appeared paler against the darkening clouds.

The last time they dunked her, she ran out of breath. She tried to curl upward to lift her head out of the sphere, but she had become weak. Fluid oozed into her ears, up her nostrils, beneath her eyelids, and coursed through her body. She heard distant voices. *Persevere and join hands with others.* Limbs untied, she reached out, bare fingers grasping still water. Her legs drew up close to her body. Curled into a ball, she spun in the briny fluid and settled into the curve of the sphere. She saw Xuan through the glassy eye.

"It's over," Xuan said and laboriously fished her out of the colossal eyeball. He carried her and ascended steps, dripping wet. *Put me down.* She wanted to resist; no words came. Sunrays from a long leaf-shaped eye shone over the great arched entrance. Except for the bullet holes that broke the exact centers of the stained-glass windows, the temple appeared intact and vivid under the lowering sky.

They crossed the threshold. Once they were inside, she heard lively conversation that became louder. She shivered uncontrollably when Xuan laid her on the cold tile floor beneath the golden light that glowed from the vaulted ceiling where people lounged on a lofty pyramid-shaped lantern. Now and then, they would glance down at her. She strained her ears to listen but could only catch fragments.

"She's rather pallid," said the woman carved from white marble to a red-haired girl. The woman was sitting coyly on a lotus blossom, her thin stone legs dangling over its petals.

"Soaked like a field mouse," Xuan mumbled and stripped off her wet clothes. He took off his shirt, and using it like a cloth, he tried to pat her dry. He pulled her hair back and placed a sweaty palm over her forehead. He then put his ear on her chest and listened for a minute. He left suddenly, his footsteps fading. Moments later when he returned, he wrapped her in a cool cottony sheet.

"I'd never be caught in yellow," the red-haired girl said to the white marble woman. She fingered her polished bob. She was suited in black armor. "Couldn't he find something else to cover her?" She hoisted her spear and leapt from the lantern onto a golden dragon. They floated across the blue starlit ceiling.

Xuan pressed hard against her chest and released, pressed and released, making her insides coil and tumble in painful waves. He pinched her nose and blew warm smoky breath into her.

"I was once a man," the marble woman said. "Did you know I was a man a thousand years ago?"

"I think I am a man; therefore, I am," claimed the chap with a head full of chestnut curls. He spoke deliberately to no one in particular.

"I'm with you. Whatever you are, I'm with you." A voice reassured him, echoing in her head, but she couldn't see the speaker. It wasn't the bald gent with an egg-shaped face, for he was arguing with another bald fellow who wouldn't look at him but peered instead into the distance. Two elders in flowing imperial gowns, half-listening to their argument, grumbled about three submissions and four virtues.

Xuan pried her mouth open and poked a finger down her throat. He straddled her and resumed pressing on her chest, hard and fast. He breathed into her mouth and scolded her for swallowing too much dead water, coaxing her not to keep it in.

The red-haired girl in black armor was playing with the dragons and piercing clusters of white clouds with her spear. The man with the egg-shaped face smirked. "To be or not to be."

"Fine words. Fine words," commended the elder in the blue imperial gown. "Then again, fine words don't necessarily mean true virtue."

"Impossible!" exclaimed the man who was peering into the distance. "Impossible without a violent revolution." He looked down at her.

She wanted to agree but her throat was blocked. Her lips trembled.

The red-haired girl was making rainclouds with the tap of her spear.

Lightning struck.

Voices thundered, and the rain came, rapping against the tile roof and glass windows, splashing cold beads onto her face.

"Accept, child. Let things go their own way. Don't impose your will on nature." A soothing voice coaxed her into a float-like sleep like a boat adrift at sea until she shuddered and coughed and waves of water surged from her body.

"Ah, the girl is awake." Xuan was sitting on his haunches beside her. He wiped the corners of her mouth with the back of his hand. "Get dressed. I'll be outside."

At the door, he called, "Nous partons, adieu Oncle!"

A Vietnamese voice croaked back, "Vous fermerez la porte, s'il vous plaît."

Maia reached for her clothes and saw the jade locket in the pile. She tore a thin strip of the yellow curtain, drew it through the locket, and tied it around her neck. She put on her damp clothes and became aware of the raw welts around her wrists and ankles.

Light slanted through the holes and cracks in the lattice windows along the walls. At the center of each window, a left eye set in a triangle stared out. Apart from an old sweeper grumbling in French about the persistent dust blown in from outside, the temple was deserted under the glowing lantern suspended from the ceiling.

Xuan's eyes fell on her locket when she emerged on the steps. "You shouldn't carry the dead with you," he said.

At the foot of the mountain, they found the Honda Dream intact, except for a missing rearview mirror. The fruit boy was nowhere in sight. The motley tents had been taken down, and the wind dispersed traces of what remained, only an imprint of the crate and camel tracks were left on the ground.

The trail along the lotus ponds through the rubber forest to the highway had turned into muddy rivulets after the rain. Xuan had not uttered a word to her since they left the mountain. He muttered to himself, his mouth moving animatedly, as if to assure his points would get across. She could not make out his speech, even leaning forward, but smelled smoke and the drizzling jungle, sometimes a musky pine.

She held onto him as they picked up speed. The wind stung the welts on her wrists and ankles. Bright colors and long leaf-shaped eyes appeared, and voices whirred in her head. Light and hollow, she slipped into the flowing surroundings along the rain-swept highway. She was a tiny tadpole twirling in a brook, a rice grain ripening in the field beyond, a raindrop on a leaf tip waiting for the sun.

She was an orphan—no link with the past, no apparent threat to the present regime. This was how the Independent Vietnam Coalition had rationalized her selection as the replacement after Vinnie Huynh's disappearance. A young woman could pass through Tan Son Nhat International Airport more easily than a man, they had predicted. Her not breaking under a second interrogation proved to them that she could detach herself from her bodily existence and be still amid the spinning world.

The ferry was set to leave when Xuan and Maia arrived at a Mekong tributary.

"Sold out," the ticket man said. "The next comes at four."

He pointed to a cluster of plastic tables and stools beneath the shadow of a tamarind tree where they could wait. On the trunk hung the vendor's menu painted in a flowing white script: *Hủ Tiếu Nam Vang, Dừa Tươi & Bia Hơi.*

They watched the last passengers boarding the ferry. They saw a marble-skinned woman and a red-haired girl. They spotted a chap with a head full of chestnut curls and a bald gentleman with an egg-shaped face and another bald fellow and two elders in blue imperial gowns. A middle-aged bearded man with a staff stood apart from the group. The motley travelers wanted free passage for their old camel and wooden crate.

"Big but not heavy," said the fruit boy from the mountain. "There's nothing inside. The empty crate floats, and Charlee swims like a swamp buffalo." The boy led the camel into the red muddy water and climbed atop her hump. They began across the river. The sun glared off the mirror in his hand. Behind them, the ferry lugged the crate that bobbed in and out the Mekong like a remnant of a shipwreck.

"Foreigners," the soup lady muttered, "finally rounded up and kicked out." She set a plate of fresh herbs, chilies, and limes on the table and offered Xuan loose imported cigarettes without names.

He had ordered three soups, two beers, and a coconut. He placed a soup, beer, and cigarettes before the empty seat between them. He fumbled in his shirt pocket for a lighter, lit a cigarette, and took a long drag.

Maia watched him from the corners of her eyes as she mixed the noodle, immersing the chopped scallion and cilantro and sliced raw onions into the steaming broth. He appeared less distant. She had first thought his name, which meant "springtime," was ironic but now seemed almost fitting. She wondered whether it was she who had changed. Maybe it was all that time in the eyeball, all that water she had drunk and coughed up. She knew enough to guard herself against him. He had taken her to the interrogation and pretended to care afterward. In spite of her caution, she felt her inside shifting, like the earth around dormant seeds about to sprout.

She realized then that he had been talking to her father's ashes.

She stirred her soup and watched a shrimp, all curled up, back slit open and tail intact, spin along the edge of the bowl. Calamari cut cylindrically and fish processed into dumplings bobbed around her bamboo chopsticks. She added fresh mint leaves and chili to the bowl, turning the broth red. The soup filled her mouth, rushed down her throat, and warmed her.

"My father doesn't smoke or drink," she said.

"His soul gets lost if you don't tell him where you're going."

A long, narrow canoe brimming with fruits and vegetables sped past them down the river to the floating market. Beyond, small thatched-roof sampans were anchored some distance apart. They were homes of those who made their living dredging silt from the delta's riverbed. On a sampan where wisps of smoke rose, a young girl on her haunches cooked the family's afternoon meal. When she stood up, the wind blew her sun-bleached clothes against her thin body and tousled her shoulder-length hair. She tilted into the wind like a carved figurehead guiding the sampan.

"During the war, we didn't sing quan hò and fall in love in the field," Xuan said. "We followed the Party's three delays."

> If you don't have a child, delay having one.
> If you aren't married, delay getting married.
> If you aren't in love, delay love.[3]

"Did you?" Maia asked.

"The trail had just been bombed," Xuan said, "so our unit spent the night at a way station. She was sixteen with eyes like longan seeds. She was scrubbing white cloths against a river boulder when we arrived. I offered her the sandalwood soap my mother had given me. She tossed me a marble stone from the river. I strung my hammock for her, but she said I needed the rest. The following night, she guided us through the jungle, white cloth flitting through the trees like fireflies."

The loud popping noise of a tugboat's engine signaled people to gather at the riverbank. They rolled up their pants legs and waded into the murky water with bundles of fruits and vegetables. A pickup truck with a mound of red dirt, an old sky blue Vanagon, motorcycles of various models, and rusty bicycles all jostled forward as the ramp lowered. Xuan pushed the Honda Dream onto the ferry, signaling her to keep close. They wedged themselves between a motorcycle with a brace of ducks tied by their feet from the handlebars and a bicycle with a basketful of rambutans on the rear rack. As the tugboat pulled the barge across the river, a cool breeze touched Maia's cheeks. The breeze bore the smells of the Nine Dragons and the people around her. Their skin, eyes, and hair resembled hers. She was among her people, yet she felt a world away.

Nearby, a blind man strummed on a recycled aluminum guitar and sang "Nắng Chiều," a prewar ballad of late afternoon light. A woman hawked bright fiery flowers, whose ethereal scent intermingled with the pungent living river. "Flowers from Sadec," she called, weaving through the crowd and coming up to Xuan. "A yellow rose for the girl?"

Xuan bought a bouquet of white chrysanthemums, which the woman wrapped in a decade-old sheet of newspaper and then placed in the Honda Dream's front basket.

"Flowers for the dead," he murmured.

They ferried across the Mekong.

Returning

"WHO'D BUY FLOWERS from the dead?"

"The dead."

"For—?"

"The living."

"Vô duyên!" the woman scolded Hai.

Slit-throat, the rooster, scatted behind the starfruit tree that shaded part of the garden from the early morning sun.

"Đi! Đi!" Hai chuckled. "She can kill you twice."

Slit-throat stretched his neck around the tree, keeping an eye on the woman.

"It's the living that buy flowers for the dead," the woman explained and continued on the pebbled footpath through the overgrown garden, a pair of butterfly shears in her hand.

"The dead should buy flowers for the living," Hai said. Crippled legs entwined in a sitting lotus, he scooted along with his bony arms, trailing his sister-in-law. The rooster followed a safe distance behind. As they approached the row of dwarf *Ochna integerrima*, each planted in a shallow earthen planter, they saw myriad green buds. "You pinched the leaves before we left!"

On a bonsai whose thick trunk bent and curved, an early blossom bloomed. The woman got on her haunches and gazed at the small yellow flower, murmuring, "Hoàng Mai."

"Luck, harmony, and balance for Lunar New Year." Hai carefully picked the twigs and dried leaves with insects from the planter and threw them onto the ground for the rooster.

The woman began to prune the miniature mai. The pair worked quietly down the row of *Ochna integerrima* amid the garden full of voices of men playing Chinese chess by the man-made fishpond, women drawing water from the well under the guava tree, and children playing hide-and-seek among the purple dragon fruit.

"Let the boys sell these at the Tết market downtown," Hai said again. "It's extra money for the road."

The woman's hand trembled with the butterfly shears in midair.

"We can transport eight bonsai in the van. One Arm, the mechanic, single-handedly fixed the van, didn't I tell you?" Hai chuckled at his own joke. "And Squinty, the driver, is only half-blind in one eye."

Sometime after the curfew siren, after Ox Alley dimmed its lights, the woman left her bed to find her way to the family's ancestral altar. She could hear Hai and the boys in the garden, loading the yellow mai flowers onto her husband's old Vanagon. Bare feet on the cold cement floor made her shiver in her thin cotton đồ bộ. In the dark she felt for the matchbox, struck a light, and burned three incense sticks. The jasmine fragrance filled the airy room. She fell on her knees, clasped her hands in prayer, and chanted.

> *Nam mô A-di-đà Phật.*
> *Nam mô A-di-đà Phật.*
> *Nam mô A-di-đà Phật.*

She had been home since the night before. Nothing was unpacked, the red basket full of jars and bottles left in a corner of the room, the furniture still covered in dust. It was three days before the Year of the Rooster.

As her prayer merged with the night sounds from the garden, the creases on her forehead relaxed. Barely thirty, she had the gravity of an older woman. After her father was imprisoned and mother became frail, she traveled between the highlands and the coast, carrying merchandise to trade. She had cared for her parents and younger sister.

Now, she had a family of her own.

Dawn blushed against the cottony sky and cast shadows across the overgrown garden. The woman's prayer grew faint. Wisps of smoke curled and disappeared as the sun rose. She felt alone, as on those nights before traveling, but then she knew she would come back to the garden, to the L-shaped house, to her husband and daughter. This time, she was leaving to follow the path of returning.

Two

A Wake

BRIGHT CIRCLES GLOWED against night shadows. The three-story house with glass windows reflecting the red evening sky seemed out of place in the wetland of the Mekong Delta.

"That's the public security chief's house," the reedy old boatman said. He tied the canoe to a nipa palm beside the dock and scrutinized Maia. "How are you related to Chief Mao, if I may ask?"

"Everyone's related," Xuan said.

The boatman held onto the mangrove to steady the canoe for them to disembark.

Na, who had arrived earlier with JP and No-No, was waiting on the dock. When she saw Xuan with the chrysanthemums, she said, "You knew?" and waved him ahead on the rickety plank boardwalk toward the house where people in white mourning gathered.

Maia felt as if she had been drawn into a stage production. The address on her grandmother's letter had led her to a garden where her childhood home had once stood, now the Winter Night Café. She had come to the River of Nine Dragons, where she was told her grandmother and aunt had relocated.

Na took her hand and led her to a redbrick well to wash up. On a nearby platform sat a large earthen jar, plastic basins, and a tin bucket with a rope to draw water. The mossy deck had room for a person to wash dishes or do the laundry and hang the clothes to dry on the line that strung from the outhouse to the wild banana grove.

"You've come just in time for your grandmother's wake," Na whispered. She helped Maia don a white hooded tunic.

An ensemble of drawn-out wails came from the house.

"Hired mourners," Na said. "The Public Security Trio. Your uncle-in-law Mao also invited a camel troupe. They pitched their tents behind the house."

In the shadows, Maia could see the outline of a camel grazing by a waterway and a small stooped figure stroking the animal's immense bowed head.

The Maos had moved from Ho Chi Minh City with both widowed mothers-in-law to the swampland, where they cultivated varieties of ornamental and edible cacti. Once a week, they returned to the city to oversee the café and altar shop. On ghost festivals, death anniversaries, and funerals, they invited neighbors and friends nearby and relatives from afar, who arrived and left the secluded lot by boat.

Shrouded in white, Maia followed Na to the house. They passed local folks in everyday clothes and the travelers in motley attire. People milled about in the marshy front yard and on the open veranda. Xuan joined JP talking with the red-haired girl and the marble-skinned woman. They stood off by the orchard that stretched from the house down to the inconstant river. The tall sprawling cacti, each planted in a mound of dirt piled up from the swamp, were laden with dragon fruit and night blooming flowers.

"She's rather pallid," Maia murmured, watching Xuan bow to the marble woman.

"That's Lady Mercy," Na said, but her eyes were on JP, who was trifling with the red-haired girl.

On a grassy hillock, a middle-aged man with a carved serpent staff spoke to the crowd. "Some passed too early; many, too late," he said. "The old orchard keeper passed at the right time." The man tapped his staff, and No-No leaped and pounced on the serpent that coiled midway around the rod. The orange kitten bit into the serpent tail, dangling back and forth like a circus acrobat before letting go.

Na left Maia in the incense-filled house.

In the living room packed with people in white hooded tunics, Comrade Ty kept time by striking the brass gong, punctuating the low rumbling of fat Pâté and the high wailing of Cross-eyed Lai. Amid the hired mourners' rhythmic howling and thick smoke lay the small withered body of her grandmother on the rosewood dining table. Maia searched for traces of familiarity. Her grandmother's mask-like face revealed nothing. She looked around at her relatives, mute figures swathed in white. How could it be that she arrived on the night of her grandmother's wake?

"She passed at the right time," the man with the serpent staff said again, coming up to her. "She'd planted the fruit of her desires." He gazed at her to see if she understood.

"What desires?" Maia asked. "For whom?"

At midnight Uncle Mao led a group of men on a bird hunt. They left in a swamp boat with flashlights and long-handled nets. JP carried a bell-shaped bamboo cage. A man boasted that he could tiptoe up to a sleeping bird and seize it with his bare fingers. Another claimed he could catch a nestling pair with a single swing of the net. Before daybreak, the men returned with a cage full of twittering birds. They covered the cage to quiet the chirping and hung it from the open veranda's ceiling. The tiny brown sparrows were to be freed after the burial at dawn.

From the house to the gravesite on the eastern edge of the dragon fruit grove was not far but could only be reached by waterway. The men carried the corpse from the living room to the dock and laid it in the canoe to be drawn by Charlee the camel.

When Mama Mao had first heard about the foreigners and their floating crate and camel crossing the Mekong River, she immediately ordered her public security chief son to escort the troupe to their home. As soon as she gazed into the camel's large eyes, broad nose, and subrident lips, she knew. "The face of a dragon!"

Mama Mao had also sensed a polyhistoric presence in the waterlogged crate and insisted that it be set in a dry well-lit room. The mammoth dripping box was hauled up the spiral stairwell to the third-floor attic and placed beside the family's ancestral altar.

That morning when the sun rose over the Mekong Delta, the camel with the dragon face ceremoniously pulled the hearse-canoe, leading a procession of sixteen small boats upstream. At the eastern front of the orchard, the mourners disembarked and proceeded in a single file to the burial site, where a princely young man in saffron rags led a chant on being freed from the illusory world.

"So fine!" Na said.

"What does he mean by *interbeing*?" Maia turned to Na. "How are all things interdependent—oneself and another, human and non-human, life and death? How is there a universe in a flower?"[4]

Na was not listening but whispering to herself. "So fine," she said again. "Too bad he's a monk."

Released at the end of the ceremony, the sparrows soared into the light that speckled their wings with indigo, crimson, and gold. The bell-shaped cage was rattled and tilted sideways to encourage a straggler that finally dropped on the ground. The injured bird was quickly kicked to a nearby cactus. The flock of sparrows trailed the procession downstream, circled the morning sky, and settled in the banana grove.

After the guest mourners left in canoes and the travelers retired to their tents to care for Charlee, who had suddenly fallen ill, those that remained gathered on the open veranda under a blanket of starlit sky.

Maia sat with her legs crossed in a half lotus, glad for the immovable hard tiles beneath her. She had not felt like herself since the eyeball interrogation. Things remained fragmented; odds and ends juxtaposed and floated in a pond of mumbo jumbo. Since arriving at her grandmother's wake, she had found herself entangled in the moment and had become a member of the cast of strangers. Perhaps if she were to let go, the events would not seem odd nor incidental but interconnected somehow. Only then, her friend Phat in Little Saigon had said, would she find a single thread and see totality. *Be still,* he would tell her. *Observe.*

Xuan leaned against the railing, a Tiger Beer in one hand. He smoked nonstop without saying a word, watching her from the corner of his eye.

JP and No-No were sprawled out on the cool tile floor. The skeletal orange kitten lay on its back, four scrawny paws in the air, a protruding bellybutton on top of a bloated stomach.

"Too much funeral food," Na said.

"He ate the dead bird." JP rubbed No-No's belly in small circles, giving the orphan kitten an after-meal lomilomi.

"It's a mark of filial piety that you've returned," Uncle Mao said, clasping Maia's hand in his firm, calloused grip. "You're a child of Vietnam."

Beside him, Auntie Mao lowered her eyes.

"She's here on research," fat Pâté chimed in, beaming. "Did you know Hòn Vọng Phu is a tale of faithful waiting?"

As if on cue, Cross-eyed Lai, who had been tuning an aluminum steel-string guitar, slap-strummed the marching rhythm of "Hòn Vọng Phu 1." Comrade Ty led off with magnificent gusto, and Pâté and Lai intoned the chorus. After the soldiers marched off to war, Na sang "Hòn Vọng Phu 2," a lyrical ballad about a wife waiting and eventually turning into stone. Na's soulful voice blended tenderly with the sparrows' night chirping.

JP scribbled in his journal. "Did her husband ever return?"

Xuan tapped his cigarette over the railing, ashes falling, his eyes on the fireflies flashing in shadows. He recited the opening lines of "Hòn Vọng Phu 3."

> *Atop the Western Range*
> *someone gazes toward the Eastern Sea,*
> *waiting—*
> *like our country from past to present.*[5]

"Why wait?" Maia asked. She felt Uncle Mao's grip and Auntie Mao's eyes.

"Your Má should have waited," Uncle Mao said quietly.

The singers fell silent. The flock of sparrows on the banana grove stopped twittering. The breeze, heavy with the smell of algae and fragrance of white nocturnal flowers, bore a mixture of sweet spices from the travelers' bonfire, where No-No had trotted off after sniffing the air. The revelers sucked in the strange scents and fell asleep full of dreams of life elsewhere.

Dewdrops

LEE HAKAKU BOYDEN taught Kai the different words for wind: *sea breeze, land breeze, easterly, westerly, monsoon,* and *typhoon*. But what Kai had a knack for was sniffing the air to tell who was near their campground. Lee and Kai would venture from their unit with gourds of jungle moonshine that Cook Cu had distilled and barter with passersby for the things they needed. Lee, a former US Army translator, spoke the Montagnard tongues, and Kai, indigenous to the mountains, could offer to clear shortcuts for travelers or guide the lost.

While Kai sniffed out what was *in* the wind, Lee smelled things from long ago, invisible things in the present, and things that had not yet happened. When the incessant easterly blew from the Central Highlands across their campground, Lee became insomniac with concern, which intensified with Vinnie Huynh's arrival, bearing news from the headquarters in Little Saigon, California.

Trained with the Special Forces, the young Vietnamese American was full of talk of *The Art of War*, reciting passages and filling Kai's ears with combat strategies and tactics such as deploying spies and incendiary attack. Vinnie also got Kai hooked on Camels, whose sweet unfiltered smoke evoked a deep familiarity Kai could neither place nor explain.

Lee, whom Kai had taken to calling "Pops," accelerated his language lessons, teaching his hānai boy all he knew: Lee's own mother tongues, the lingoes he had learned formally in school and picked up in Kalihi Valley, and those he had cultivated to survive the jungles of Southeast Asia. Lee convinced Kai of the importance of language, through which one encountered the other in the world. Knowing languages was a hingeless door that swung in all directions, a pivot on which one stood to see intersecting horizons in order to understand oneself as another.

"To live is to speak and to listen," Lee would say. "Life's a conversation. Spiders spin webs, trees fruit, and birds sing. They're speaking. Listen."

To Lee's chagrin, Kai picked up tweeting most readily. The pair would spend time carving birdcalls from jungle materials to imitate the mountain babblers. More and more, Pops and son twittered, conversing with each other and their surroundings in nature's intimate codes.

Lee suspected the transformation was brought about by Cook Cu's jungle moonshine: dried leaves, berries, barks, and other nameless ingredients, steeped in morning dew. A descendant of the royal poet-chef for the fourth Nguyen Emperor, Cook Cu concocted a mountain dew that induced the men to become one with the wilderness. On the other hand, his nightly poetry recital from memory of his ancestral *Gia Phả Họ Kim* transported them to another time and place.

"Dewdrops," from his family annals, was a favorite of Cook Cu's.

Frangipani and a grove of pine lap about the crumbling stones
that celebrate Tu Duc, the ineffable, the longest reigning Nguyen emperor,
and no wonder, breezes whisper—
             he lived.

At every meal, fifty chefs stewed and boiled, steeped and steamed,
crafted fifty cunning dishes, served by fifty trembling servants;
no need to tell what sudden fate awaited

> *fumbling feet.*
>
> *His tea was made from drops of dew gathered from the lotus petal,*
> *shadows moving in the shallows round the teahouse, every dawn*
> *five hundred quivering beads to make*
> > *a perfect pot.*
>
> *That much the almanac reveals but not what sort of perfect flowers,*
> *only dewdrops from the petals of young maidens,*
> *the trembling dew of blushing lotus*
> > *filled the pot.*[6]

Progressively paralyzed by his ailment, Cook Cu strove for inner stillness. His moonshine induced a drunken forgetfulness among the men so as to be in the present. His nightly poetry recital stirred them to take flight to a life elsewhere.

Vinnie's arrival jolted the stasis.

Lee sensed restlessness in Kai, who began to venture with Vinnie beyond the campground's perimeter and would not return for days. Lee's suspicion that they were crossing the border into Vietnam's Central Highlands was confirmed when he overheard them conversing with one another in tribal animal-like calls. After more than two decades in the jungle, Lee had come to a crossroad. The child he had carried from the burning rubble of war had not physically grown but was now overflowing with action.

The Dead Letter Box

THE ROOSTERS WOKE Maia from a restless night the morning after the burial. The house was nearly deserted. Except for the travelers caring for their sick camel, almost everyone had gone for the day. Na had convinced JP to accompany her to Sadec to scout a location for a café. Chief Mao, in a crisp public security uniform, reported to Station House 49. Auntie Mao, the town's postmistress, rode with him in the family canoe to her one-woman post office.

That left Mama Mao. Before making her weekly trip to oversee her altar shop in Ho Chi Minh City, the old woman enlisted Maia to help with preparing a fruit offering. The bowed figure in brown cotton clothes led Maia to the surrounding trees.

"Mâm ngũ quả," she instructed.

They picked a spiny dragon fruit, a red pomegranate, a hand of plump bananas, a fragrant pomelo, and a nipa palm nut. They arranged and re-arranged the five fruits on the round lacquer tray until Mama Mao sighed approvingly. "Balance and harmony."

Maia carried the tray and trailed the old woman up into the attic. As they climbed the spiral stairwell, Mama Mao instructed Maia to light incense for her ancestors. "Remember, bow your head and don't stare." When they reached the landing, the old woman took the offering and approached the wooden crate, where water had seeped out onto the floor. Maia followed closely behind.

"Stand back," Mama Mao hissed. "You light incense." The old woman placed the offering on the floor before the crate and fell on her knees. She sniffed the water, dipped an arthritic finger into the puddle, and licked its crooked tip, tongue moving in toothless mouth. "The Mekong River," she muttered. She dipped another finger but this time sucked it like a lollipop. "Saltier," she said, "like the ocean." She mumbled something about an early nineteenth century shipwreck in the middle of the Atlantic, trying to retrace the passage of the cargo with her tongue.

Mama Mao prostrated before the wooden crate and chanted in a high voice that filled the silence and stilled Maia's breath. The box contracted and expanded, and a dull pounding pulsated from within. Maia held her breath and watched the old woman and box unblinkingly until she realized it was her own heart beating. She released her breath and took several steps back. She calmed herself and scanned the bare attic. On the family altar, framed black-and-white photographs of different sizes and shapes crowded under the red glow of the electric candlelight. She approached the altar, feeling the eyes on her and remembering Mama Mao's words: *bow your head and don't stare.*

Maia lit three incense sticks. Wisps of jasmine smoke spiraled upward and lingered in the stagnant air. She bowed three times. When she stuck the joss sticks into the sandy miniature planter, she could not help but peek at her ancestors' faces. All seemed to be strangers. Her eyes then rested on a four-by-six-inch unframed picture, dusty and curling at the edges. Tucked in a corner of the altar, Great-Aunt Tien gazed out: an open smile, wild long hair, and skin the color of her black clothes. Beside her great-aunt stood an older man—pale, thin, and a wispy beard.

"Don't stare," Mama Mao said.

"That's, that's—"

"Your side of the family."

"She's alive . . . isn't she? And . . . is that . . . Uncle Ho?"

Mama Mao picked up the picture, glanced at the pair, and turned it over. Still sucking on her tongue, she scrutinized the inscription and then handed the picture to Maia. "You read." They moved toward the circular glass window for more light. The writing had faded, but Maia could still make out the words. There was no date. "You can read Vietnamese, can't you?" Mama Mao asked.

In the cylindrical beam of sunlight through the attic window, Maia slowly read the words out loud.

> *Núi ấp ôm mây, mây ấp núi*
> *Lòng sông gương sáng bụi không mờ*
> *Bồi hồi dạo bước Tây Phong Lĩnh*
> *Trông lại trời Nam, nhớ bạn xưa.*
> —H.C.M.[7]

"It's a poem," Maia said. "For my great-aunt . . . from Uncle Ho?"

"Who knows?" Mama Mao shrugged. "Would you like to see more family pictures?" Not waiting for an answer, the old woman fell on her knees and opened the cabinet doors beneath the altar. Raising dust clouds and disregarding spider webs, she pulled out an antique cookie tin and extended it to Maia. "This is for you."

A soft morning glow illuminated the verdant swampland. Maia placed the tin box on the tile veranda and sat in the shadow cast by the extended roof. The river had flooded the dock and reached far up the front yard below the house. No-No trotted up from the wet grass, where he had been basking in the sunbeam. He pressed his bony head against her leg and coiled his rat-like tail around her ankle. He plopped on his side, exposing a distended belly for her to rub.

Dust rose and spun in the slanted morning light as Maia opened the tin to find an old photograph of her parents. Her mother smiled, head tilted, half-shut eyes gazing at her father, who stared at her, holding her hand and grinning widely. They stood in the garden of the L-shaped house in a world of their own. Maia came across a picture of her father in olive drabs, hoisting a rifle and leaning against a stone bridge. With an oversize helmet on his head and a hand grenade hanging on his flak jacket, he looked like a teenager dressed up in someone else's uniform. Behind him, the bridge arched across the river like a crescent moon.

Beneath the pictures, she found a bundle of several letters. She recognized her father's even and deliberate handwriting. A yellowing page, torn from a notebook, addressed her father in a hasty scrawl. It was a letter from her mother, the date and location illegible. Maia returned the box to the altar's cabinet and kept the letters, suspecting they never reached the intended readers.

She followed the overgrown footpath into the dragon fruit grove. Veering toward the sound of rushing water, she came to a clear river lined with weeping willows. Large floating leaves spread from bank to bank, covering the river in green except where blushing pink lotuses bloomed. She tucked herself under the shade of a willow and began to read a letter from her father to her mother.

I've been waiting for your letter but nothing has arrived. This evening, live bands performed on the corners of downtown Philadelphia to welcome the summer's arrival. In the midst of the festivity, I felt the warmth of my tears.

What is the meaning of a cluster of evening clouds, a yellow leaf windblown from the past autumn, or a gentle breeze from the rose garden of Sadec where we stopped for a meal of fish and vegetables?

You were always away. I waited for you like the rose garden from yesteryear still waiting for your return. On those rainy evenings at the train station, I watched passengers disembark. After waiting, I could only help you with the bags.

I was mad at the clouds. I blamed the wind. I even hated the yellow autumn leaf.

Visiting you on the nights when the town was bustling, the most we ever did was accompanying others out. Why didn't we make a date on one of those evenings to go to the lake atop the mountain? The trail, though not spectacular, did have the gentle breeze whispering through the pines. With you beside me, I'd see your hair blowing in the wind, hold your hand in mine, and hear your voice. We'd have had a chance to talk about a life that matters.

I still haven't seen a more beautiful footpath than the one along the open marketplace beyond the bridge. Then, we were living at Old Lady B, sharing house with Captain V, who wanted to fire his gun in the middle of the night. After that, we rented a house from Sister L behind the wooden church.

Do you still remember the rooster that I asked you not to sacrifice? You didn't know how much I loved him. He never pecked at your mother's flowerpots. He'd follow me everywhere. Whenever he heard me calling, wherever he was, he'd come running. But I had to carry out your wish. That night, I couldn't sleep and woke at three in the morning. I embraced him . . .

Fragments of memory emerged. Bits and pieces of a childhood with her father in Philadelphia floated to the surface, a life of incidents she had not reconciled but submerged in the sea of forgetting. As the flotsam of her family's private lives resurfaced, she began to wonder how she was led to march to the expatriates' drumbeat. Her love for her father, an ARVN soldier who fought for the South, moved her to participate in the continual fight for Vietnam's freedom. The banner of democracy for all Vietnamese comforted the exiles like a security blanket in a foreign land, under which they dreamed of one day returning home.

LOVE Park

IN THE CITY of Brotherly Love, Maia's father rode a secondhand bicycle everywhere. On icy wintry streets, in cool spring air, and muggy summer days, he pedaled. The orderly and smooth concrete streets—oh, how different from his homeland. He biked to adult English class, to the public library, to auto mechanic retraining, to the market for fruits and vegetables and pig intestines and oxtails and chicken feet.

Once, at the Italian Market on South Ninth Street, he bought a whole chicken live. His hands waved to the butcher: "No, no! Don't cut throat!" It was a red hen to replace the rooster that had followed him everywhere in a garden from long ago. A keepsake of things past, the red hen freely roamed the upstairs.

Once on a windy, rainy autumn night, he came home from his class—excited, nervous, and proud. In a brown Acme paper bag in his bicycle front rack were two squabs, wet and scared, squawking for their mother.

His bicycle also had a rear rack for Maia. In the summer, in the morning hours when streetlamps still lit the neighborhood in a soft yellow glow, they would ride to Broad Street and Passyunk Avenue. They waited with other farm workers to bus to New Jersey's blueberry fields.

The summer she was twelve, she became aware of her changing body. She was glad for those days of open fields and clear skies and the boys who teased her. They teased her walk as she balanced heavy blueberry crates on her shoulder. In their gazes, her tomboy swag became a swing of hips.

In those green fields—muddy from the night rain, wet and mosquito-infested at dawn, and a blazing sun at noon— she experienced the freedom of working for one's keep. The changes went unobserved before the dresser mirror in the apartment cluttered with secondhand knickknacks and old memories. Away from the concrete inner-city neighborhood, among the open fields beneath the lofty skies, she first glimpsed a self-propelling wheel turning from within.

When she said she picked blueberries in Jersey, someone would respond, "Blueberry Hill?" and lapse into Fats Domino. "I found my thrill—on Blueberry Hill—"

She listened, but the thrill of her first kiss was at LOVE Park.

"Can I kiss you?" he had asked. They were sitting on a frozen bench, watching downtown early morning traffic. She was a high school senior, working two jobs. She had never been kissed, and he was a stranger almost twice her age, a homeless man. He was slouching on the park bench beside her. "Why look so sad?" He pulled off the hood of his tattered sweatsuit, smiling a *wanna-talk?*

She had felt invisible amid the concrete space of center city—its gray buildings, passing cars sealed against the frigid December air, and people in business attire. The man on the adjacent bench spoke. He patted the space next to him, and she came. She did not want to go home to the apartment, to a cave-like closet turned bedroom packed with used books, amidst which her ailing father slept, dreaming of Saigon and the wife he'd left behind. Sometimes nightmares of war jolted him awake, sweating in the stillness of a wintry morning.

The man said he stayed at a place nearby. Where did she live? He was married and had an adolescent daughter. How old was she? Why look so sad?

She could not tell him about the decisions she had to make—staying home with her father or leaving for college. He would not understand. If she were awarded a scholarship, she would have enough for a one-way Greyhound fare and new running shoes. The college had beautiful cross-country trails, the brochure advertised, and a supportive all-women environment.

The park bench was cold. "What about you," she asked, "why are you sad?"

"Me?" He took a swig from the bottle in a paper bag. "Want some?" His breath smelled of sweet minty licorice.

She shook her head.

"When I came back from 'Nam," he paused, "my wife didn't want to see me, didn't want me to see our girl."

"My father was in the war, too."

"She remarried," he said, crossing his legs at the ankles. He wore scruffy Nike sneakers.

"Do you run? Nikes are this year's top running shoes."

"I stopped running. Too humid, dusty, polluted even at four in the morning, couldn't goddamn breathe, not to mention Charlie's punji traps, toe-poppers, feces-smeared spikes." He gulped down the bottle. "Sure wanna start again." He wiped the greenish liquid from his mouth with the back of his hand. "The place I'm staying opens at five," he said. "We're on our own during the day. You can stop by."

"I can't. I work. From four to eleven, I work at a Japanese teppanyaki house in Bala Cynwyd. I'm a hostess. I wear a purple silk kimono from Japan. I work the graveyard shift at Dunkin' Donuts in North Philly."

"Can I kiss you?"

The kiss did not make her feel dizzy or weak like a heroine in a Harlequin Romance, nothing like those first kisses her classmates swooned over at lunchtime. She had kissed other lips since. She sought those who ran in full strides, who had not stumbled in war, who laughed at Charlie Brown. But she never forgot her first kiss from an American who had been in 'Nam.

A Prison Letter

THE WEEPING WILLOW draped like a curtain around Maia. She did not realize she was not alone until she heard murmuring and saw uniformed legs through the wind-blown branches. She quickly folded the letters and tucked them into a crevice under the roots that had grown above ground. She slipped out from beneath the canopy, over the riverbank, and into the water. Where she slid in, the lilies scattered and then slowly returned. By the time the men came and stood under the willow, the river was evenly covered again with blushing pink lotuses and expansive emerald pads from bank to bank.

As her feet hit bottom, she pulled her legs up and rolled forward. Hands clasped and then extended, she dolphin kicked beneath the water lilies and swam away from the bank. The hum of the river enveloped her. Her heart pounded with urgency as if ready to burst. She rotated onto her back and grabbed onto the rootstalks to keep from surfacing. When she lifted her mouth through a gap between the leaves to gulp in air, she saw Xuan and the Public Security Trio scanning the area. They exchanged words she could not hear. They retreated through the dragon fruit grove.

She floated in the river among the lilies, waiting for her heartbeat to slow. Her father's letter had opened a floodgate of yearning that had been kept shut as they tried to rebuild their lives in America. When she left the river, she welcomed the warmth of the late afternoon. After some time under the sun, squeezing water from her clothes and untangling twigs and dead leaves and bugs from her hair, she settled again in the shadow of the weeping willow and retrieved the letters from the crevice. Reading several more letters from her father to her mother, Maia realized the isolation she felt while growing up in Philadelphia was in part because of her father's sense of defeat. Escaping to America was not the beginning of a new life for him, but a coda to a life unlivable in his homeland, yet impossible elsewhere.

She came to the yellowing page torn from a notebook, her mother's letter to her father.

> *I've been here for eight months and have written to you twice. I asked my sister to mail the letters. Have you received them?*
>
> *For the past months, I was sent out to clear forests, plow fields, and plant crops. Each inmate is assigned an eighty-by-one-meter strip. In the morning when the sky is cool, the plowing isn't bad, but in the afternoon, the heat makes it hard to breathe. Day after day, our work continues.*
>
> *Recently, my duties have changed. I've been reassigned to the kitchen. There are ten of us: head chef, assistant chef, two pig caretakers, and six cooks, of which I'm one. I get up every morning at 4:30, divide the rice portions, carry water from the well, rinse the rice, boil four pots of water, and cook six pots of rice and vegetables for the whole day. At dawn, I carry vegetables from the field to the kitchen. At noon, I carry rice from the granary to the kitchen. The work is hard, especially sifting rice and bringing water in from the well, but not as hard as working in the field under the scorching sun.*
>
> *Writing to you, I'm reminded of the time when we first met and the time we were away from each other. Already it's been more than ten years—a period that seems long and far away, yet it also seems like yesterday. I've been a wife and a mother, but have I completed my duties?*
>
> *Please don't worry about me. Whatever situation I'm put into, I'll stay composed and wait for the day to see you again.*

I'll be brave and look straight ahead. I'm ready to accept what's handed to me. Your love has been enough in the past and will be enough for the days to come even if I don't see you again.

As the missing pieces fell into place, more questions arose. Why was her mother in prison? During those years apart, her parents' letters had never reached one another but were collected in a dead letter box. Why?

It was evening when Maia left the riverbank to find the path back to the house. Tree branches rustled and shadows of laundry drying on the line wavered in the breeze. The songs of crickets, frogs, and birds filled the night. She listened for movements but only heard the crunching of pebbles beneath her feet and the slow creak of the plank when she stepped on the platform beside the well. She pulled at the rope that hung over the edge of the well and retrieved a bucket of water. She stripped, got onto her haunches and rinsed the mud off her shirt and pants, and then hung them to dry on the line. She fetched another bucket and poured the cool water over herself, washing the river's debris from her hair, its crusty film on her skin, the dried silt between her toes. Standing under the quarter moon, all around her was a blur. "What if Má were still alive?" she whispered. That night, she felt closer to her mother than any of those nights when she gazed at the moon on the other side of the world.

"Be brave," Má had said. "Look at the moon and you'll see me."

They huddled with others by the riverbank in the dark. Her mother held her hand, her father their few belongings. They were waiting to be taken to the big boat to cross the South China Sea.

In the distance, bright paper lanterns dangled to and fro, illuminating shadows of children celebrating the Mid-Autumn Festival of 1978.

When the outlines of two small boats appeared, she grabbed onto her mother's slender finger and they waded together into the river mouth. The women and children were led toward one boat, the men toward the other. Standing in the water, her mother passed her to her father and bade him to board with the women and children. The middlemen objected until her mother climbed into the boat with the men that never made it out to sea.

The Be River

"Somewhere before the Be River empties into Lake Waterfall Dreams," Auntie Mao said, "you'll find the prison. Your Má was held there after you and your Ba escaped."

"Why weren't the letters sent? Who kept them under the altar?"

Auntie Mao evaded Maia's questions. "Your Má had more than a few suitors. It's regrettable she chose your Ba."

When the roosters crowed at dawn, Maia and Na bid goodbye to JP, who had decided to stay with the motley troupe to care for the dying camel. He wanted to explore the nearby underground tunnels he had read about. Maia sensed it was more than just an interest in history but did not ask, nor did he pry about her hasty departure and lent his motorcycle readily. Na had agreed to accompany Maia without any explanation beyond sightseeing. The two women borrowed JP's used Minsk and returned to Ho Chi Minh City on National Highway 1. From the city, they followed the Dong Nai River northward to the Be River.

Maia and Na took turns driving. They stopped early for a breakfast of phở and iced coffee along the way and then for gas and a lunch of cơm bình dân later. They followed the Be River until late afternoon when it crossed Route 13 and continued westward toward Cambodia. When they finally stopped at a roadside diner to ask for directions, they learned that they had left the Be River a while back and were following a provincial stream. They were advised to take Route 13, which ran parallel to the Cambodian border, for about ten more kilometers to the village Loc Ninh, where they could find a place to spend the night and set out again in the morning.

The roadside diner, a long rectangle with rough concrete floor and white plastic tables and chairs, was deserted except for a group of timber truckers. The owner's young twin daughters led the women through the diner, past the family's cramped living quarters, to the well in the backyard to wash up. The eatery fronted the noisy and dusty thoroughfare to draw travelers. The back opened to acres and acres of lush coffee fields and a pine-fringed horizon.

On the table when they returned were stewed catfish with pork belly, bitter melon soup, and steamed white rice. At the next table a sunburnt trucker eyed them. He downed his iced draft beer and spoke loudly to his companion.

"Saigonese don't come up this way."

"My neighbor was traveling to the highlands last month," his friend said, picking his teeth with a splinter, "when a group of FULRO rebels hijacked the bus and robbed everyone. The *Công An News* reported that they raped two passengers."

"You don't have to worry about that." The first man snorted. "But if the highlands are sealed off again, that would be inconvenient for business."

After dinner, Maia and Na were upset to find that they had a flat tire. They tried not to suspect foul play as they pushed the motorcycle from the diner, following the twins' lead off Route 13 onto a dirt road to an open market. Among the fruit stalls, vegetable stands, and baskets of herbs and grains, they saw a shrunken old man sitting on a wooden

box with an eroded air pump set before him. On the bicycle behind him hung a small cardboard sign advertising
Sửa Xe. He beckoned.

They left the Minsk with the repairman and wandered
through the marketplace. The smell of deep-fried shrimp
and mung bean patties from a bánh cuốn stall filled the
air. The vendor in a lilac đồ bộ waved customers to her foot-
stools and knee-high tables as she served plates of steamed
rice rolls filled with pork mince and wood ear mushrooms,
garnished with blanched bean sprouts, fresh mint leaves,
and chili fish sauce.

Merchants squatting on their haunches hawked their
wares in woven baskets. The two women stopped at a sundry stall where Na bargained for dust masks, sun gloves, rain
ponchos, a vial of White Flower Balm, and a dozen lacy un-
derpants in assorted sizes and styles. Na, wearing a tank top,
tight-fitting jeans, and high heels, gave the impression of a
well-to-do spendthrift foreigner. The vendor quoted prices
much higher than what she finally settled for when she realized Na was as savvy a bargainer as any local Vietnamese.

After stopping at a dessert stand for warm banana tapio-
ca with coconut cream, they returned to pay the repairman
for the patched tire, but now the Minsk would not start.
When asked what was wrong, the old man shook his head
and shrugged. He packed up his tools in the wooden box,
secured it to his bicycle rear rack, and pedaled away.

Na kicked the immobile cycle. "JP got a clunker!"

The women circled the heap of inert metal as if viewing
the dead. They flanked the Minsk and shook it back and
forth, causing gasoline to drip from its teardrop tank. The
motorcycle stood nonchalantly, its headlight staring at
them like an oversized glass eye.

Maia questioned her plan. After finding the prison, Na was going to return to Ho Chi Minh City on the Minsk, and Maia would catch an express shuttle to continue to the Central Highlands. But now what? The glass eye stared at her unblinkingly. How could they have gotten lost following the Be River? Where did they miss the turn?

They were just short of wailing when a rugged dark-skinned man with wavy hair approached. He offered to give them a lift to Loc Ninh. He had a large wooden boat-like cart attached to his three-wheel motorcycle, which could transport the Minsk. He had just dropped off his last delivery for the day and was shopping for food.

When the women agreed, the young man left his trike motorcycle and boat-cart with them and disappeared into the marketplace. Moments later he returned with a case of Angkor Beer, two kilograms of escargots, pig intestines, anchovies, fresh chilies, and herbs. He had ordered a block of ice that a girl would deliver around midnight on her bicycle rear rack.

"A drinking party," he announced, adding that he lived with his mother. They had a di văng if Maia and Na needed a place for the night.

Several hundred yards off Route 13, the cartman stopped at a longhouse nestled under coconut palms. In the front yard, an old woman was rinsing a large pot of glutinous rice beside the well. Surrounding her were woven baskets of husked split mung beans, shredded coconut, and fresh pandan leaves.

"My mother sells xôi at the market in the morning," the man said.

The old woman glanced up at them, smiled, and continued picking out the stones and debris from the basket of dried beans.

"Chào bác," Na said and then followed the man to find an outhouse.

Maia sat on her haunches and joined the woman in her picking, gathering the stones with her thumb and forefinger, tucking several into her palm before scattering them. Besides a creaky bicycle passing by on the dirt road or the occasional roar of a motorcycle in the distance, only the wind ruffled the stillness.

"Ở đây rất yên tĩnh," Maia said. The old woman smiled, showing black lacquered teeth stained with red betel nut juice. Strands of white hair escaped from beneath her loose blue turban. After rinsing the mung beans, she handed Maia a basket of pandan leaves to wash. "Bác nấu xôi gì vậy?" Maia asked.

"She doesn't speak Vietnamese," the man said, returning from a shower. He spoke to his mother in an indigenous tongue and then said to Maia, "She'll show you where to sleep tonight."

With a kerosene lamp, the old woman led Maia and Na into the longhouse to a plank-bed next to the window that looked out into the front yard. She swept the dust off with a pillow and released the sides of the mosquito net. She dimmed the lamp and left it on the family's altar.

Maia and Na crawled under the mosquito net. They exhaled as soon as their backs touched the polished plank đi văng. On the thick wooden beam that ran across the A-frame ceiling, they could see a carved inscription in the flickering kerosene light. They read the words in unison like two schoolchildren.

Đồng bào Kinh hay Thổ, Mường hay Mán,
Gia-rai hay Ê-đê, Xê-đăng hay Ba-na
và các dân tộc thiểu số khác
đều là con cháu Việt Nam, đều là anh em ruột thịt.
—H.C.M.[8]

"Do you believe that people in the lowlands and high-lands are brothers and sisters, all children of Vietnam?" Na yawned and turned on her side, her back to Maia. "What would Nobodaddy say about a half-blood?"

"That's the creation myth, isn't it? Fifty children on the mountain, fifty in the sea?"

Na seemed to be asleep.

Maia lay awake, watching the evening sky through the window, remembering the man in her great-aunt's photograph and the initials H.C.M. She was now convinced that he was none other than Ho Chi Minh. She recalled the poem penned on the back of the photograph.

Mountains enfold clouds, clouds mountains,
The river heart a faithful mirror.
Restlessly wandering the Western Range,
I look back at southern skies, missing old friends.

Great-Aunt Tien and Uncle Ho. How did they know each other? What was their relationship?

"Hey, girl," a voice called softly through the window. "Are you awake? Come join us!"

She closed her eyes and pretended to be asleep. She kept count of those who came through the gate that squeaked and rattled like a timeworn accordion on its last legs. One by one, the guests greeted the host in an inaudible minority tongue. The men feasted and afterward fell into a hushed conversation. She did not understand the content but heard fervor in their voices. She suspected that she and Na had traveled into an area where the remaining members of the Front Unifié pour la Libération des Races Opprimées continued to operate. Sometime during the night, she realized Na had gotten up and gone out. She peeked through the window at the group of men sitting cross-legged on the dirt ground. Na sat with them. They were young and old but all appeared strong and resilient, conversing across the fire that still burned bright.

Mother Medium

MAIA'S NIGHT WAS full of voices that vanished when Na woke her. The voices had clarity in her dream but their meanings now blurred. Na had not slept, yet she seemed wide-awake.

They explored the empty longhouse and surroundings and ate the mung bean glutinous rice wrapped in banana leaves that were left on the table for them. They found the Minsk fixed and a note on its teardrop tank: *Follow Route 14 southward if lost.*

From Loc Ninh, they rode eastward along the watercourse and arrived at Lake Waterfall Dreams. "Is there a prison somewhere before the Be River empties into Lake Waterfall Dreams?" Maia asked the man at the hydropower plant. As soon as she repeated Auntie Mao's words aloud, Maia realized she needed more details. After whispering these directions, Auntie Mao had only added, "I visited your mother once, and that was over ten years ago."

"The Be River flows from north to south," the hydro-power plant worker corrected Maia, "from Lake Waterfall Dreams through the southeastern provinces. You're lost, aren't you?"

He pointed them to Route 14.

When the Ho Chi Minh Trail was renovated after the war, people began to settle along the newly paved thorough-fare. Route 14, an alternative to National Highway 1 on the coastline, connected the South and North through the

Central Highlands. The former trails of human sacrifice now attracted resettlement, local businesses, and international golf course development.

Following Route 14 southward, they passed roadside eateries, garden cafés, sundry stores, bicycle and motorcycle repair shops, and building supply factories. There were gas stations with adjacent bright castle-like homes and gold shops with lit-up display glass cases. They passed houses that were shacks, others were bare redbrick, and some had sleek wrap-around tiled porches. Open doorways and curtainless windows faced the thoroughfare.

Na steered the Minsk off Route 14 and onto a red dirt path cutting through lush fields of coffee, black pepper, and durians. Away from the main access were mostly thatched huts. They passed a woman on a bicycle, whose face was shaded by a straw cone hat. They went by an old man pedaling a rickshaw with a heap of wilting root vegetables in the front wooden cart. They sped by people carrying baskets full of assorted wares, all walking toward the main road.

They came upon the edge of a rubber plantation. The paved road leading into the cultivated area was wide enough for large vehicles. Everything lay in shadow under the canopy of rubber trees, whose trunks were slashed diagonally about four feet above the ground, where metal pipes had been inserted to drain the latex into half bowls. They passed a truck with three large metal tanks and came upon a group of workers. When asked for directions to the prison, no one knew. The workers' accents told them they were from northern provinces. Following the road, Maia and Na emerged from the plantation onto another dirt path, looping back to Route 14.

At a one-pump gas station, they learned that the prison had been closed. The station's owner, the town's highest-ranking official, pointed to the rubber forest as the prison's former location.

"Mother is ready!" the official's wife called from the brick house behind the station. Through the open door, Maia and Na could see people huddling in the living room, transfixed by a white robed dwarf sitting in a lotus pose.

A battered van swerved along Route 14. A young girl swung from its open side door, slapping on the metal panel to clear motorists and pedestrians from the van's path. The van came to a stop at the station, and the girl leaped off and scurried in her flip-flops to open the back door for an old woman. The girl scaled barefoot atop the vehicle, untied a large covered basket, and balanced it on the woman's turbaned head. The woman hastened away, anticipating the afternoon storm.

"Going to the Central Highlands?" the girl called, grabbing Maia's bag.

Maia pulled back on the bag.

The girl held on. "Buôn Ma Thuột? Pleiku? Kon Tum?"

"Hurry!" Na pulled Maia's arm the other way toward the house. "The dwarf is going to mediate with the dead!"

When the driver beeped the horn, the girl let go of Maia's bag and chased after the van, jumping on as it set out northward for the highlands.

Inside the house, red electric candlelight from the altar lit the living room. A six-foot-high shelf, the altar extended from wall to wall and displayed two gilded portraits: an elderly couple in traditional Chinese gowns and skullcaps, and a young man in a heavily decorated uniform of the People's Army. The young man had the same fine features as the town official.

The dwarf climbed onto the table that had been pushed against the wall beneath the altar. He stood no more than three feet tall but now gazed directly into the eyes of the old couple and young man. The town official remained beside the dwarf, waiting for directions.

"They were comrades-in-arms during the war," someone whispered. "He was escorted from the City of the Soaring Dragon."

Smoke from burning incense filled the room. People shuffled sideways, forming two single files, their backs against the wall. The town official beckoned the first woman to approach and told her to address the dwarf as *Mẹ*.

Na's eyes were glued to the altar. Maia watched the solemn ritual while listening to the rain outside. Another express van heading to the highlands stopped for fuel.

"Mẹ," said the young woman, palms clasped and eyes looking up, "when is the appropriate time for me to remarry?"

The dwarf replied in a high female voice from the back of his throat, "The eighth month of the Lunar Year of the Water Monkey."

"Mẹ," asked a thin man, "what is the course of the lotus, the palm, and the desert?"

"You play ball—rough and hard."

When Na's turn came, she spoke softly so that no one but the dwarf could hear. He placed his big hand on her left breast and responded in a barely audible whisper, "With you."

The earnestness loosened Maia's guard, and the question she had carried since she left Vietnam as a child with her father surfaced. "Thưa Mẹ, má con bây giờ ở đâu?"

The room became a blur in the haze of incense smoke. The dwarf lit a leaf of paper money and waited for it to burn. After gazing into the faces of the old dead and the young dead, he drew on a square sheet of paper at length with wild gestures.

He held it over the flame. A corner began to curl and darken, but before the sheet caught fire, loud gurgling rose from the dwarf's stomach, and his eyes rolled uncontrollably, showing their whites. He fell off the table onto the tile floor with a thud. His body convulsed, his hand still clutching the square sheet of blackened paper.

Women gathered around him, untied his robe, and rubbed White Flower Balm on his body, from his broad chest downward. Fragrances of camphor, wintergreen, and eucalyptus filled the air. A woman massaged his short legs and big feet, another his arms and hands. The dwarf stopped convulsing, his breathing long and deep.

Someone gasped. Another giggled.

"Flip him over," Na ordered the group, and they quickly turned the dwarf onto his stomach. A few proceeded to knead his muscly buttocks and thighs. Na directed two young women to carry the dwarf from the room. Maia got up to follow.

"You stay." A man grabbed her hand.

The television and VCR were pushed back into the corner, and a karaoke bar with large speakers was set up. Women entered with round aluminum trays of food, and men lugged in cases of Tiger Beer, snake wine, moonshine made from glutinous rice, and a block of melting ice. A clay charcoal stove was placed at the center of the room. The official's wife lit the charcoal briquettes, fanned them to a slow burn, and began grilling dried squids, fresh mussels, and a snakehead wrapped in banana leaves.

"What's your business at the prison?" the man asked Maia.

"I'm just visiting." She kept her eyes on the doorway where Na and the women had exited with the dwarf.

"You look like Đêm Đông," he said.

"'Winter Night'—the song?"

"An inmate. You two could be related."

Maia turned toward him.

"I delivered beer and cigarettes to the prison guards," he said. "There was a woman called Đêm Đông because each night you could hear her sing 'Winter Night' in her cell. You have her eyes." He hummed a few bars and gazed at her. "The warden was in love with Đêm Đông. The last I heard he opened a nightspot in Ho Chi Minh City and called it the Winter Night Café."

Past midnight, Maia and Na huddled outside the one-pump gas station, waiting for daylight. They had refused the town official's invitation to crash on the living room floor with other intoxicated guests. Instead, they propped themselves against the pump under the drizzling rain and a waning crescent moon.

"Time for yourself," the Independent Vietnam Coalition had agreed, "to visit family and resolve whatever questions you might have. Whatever you do, be at the Vong Phu Mountain on the first night of the full moon."

This time for herself had not resolved anything but only made her more confused. Route 14 would take her to the peak via Buon Ma Thuot. But Ho Chi Minh City beckoned. She wanted to confront Uncle Mao.

Na, glowing after leaving the dwarf, looked blissfully vacant.

"Why did you carry him from the room?" Maia asked.

Na smiled.

"Oh no," Maia said. "Don't tell me."

Na lifted her face, closed her eyes, and opened her mouth to catch the cool raindrops.

"Okay," Maia said. "Did you . . . ? Is it true that . . . ?"

"It's so hot, Mai." Na gathered her long wavy hair and twisted it into a loose knot. "Are you cold? You should've come with us, the girls and me. It opens and vibrates and releases you to our *inter-be*. JP said that you're—" Something fell from Na's bra. "Oh, here." She handed Maia a crumbled piece of singed paper.

"What did JP say?" Maia smoothed the wrinkled square on which the dwarf had made an elaborate drawing.

"Oh, I forget." Na flicked her hand. "He doesn't understand you."

"No, he doesn't."

"Can you read that?"

Maia examined the script of overlapping characters. She could not tell whether they were Chinese, Sino-Vietnamese, Cyrillic, or a combination of all those scripts. The writing was indecipherable.

"Mother said my father is with me," Na said.

"Your mother said your father is with you?"

"No. Mother Medium, the dwarf, said my father's here."

"In Vietnam?"

Na took Maia's hand and placed it on her chest. "He's *here*."

They listened to the wind howling through the deserted streets.

After a long silence, Maia said, "My father is with me, too. I have his ashes."

"Now I understand," Na said. "Your father, I saw him, a big black man."

"My father's Vietnamese, a small man with light skin."

"No. No. I saw a big black man with you the first time you walked into the café with JP."

"Sing us a song, Na. Sing us 'Đêm Đông.'"

In the early morning, Na sang of an evening that had not gone, yet the night curtain had fallen. She sang of a winter night on which a soldier longed for his homeland, a wife waited across the river, a poet listened to his soul, and a singer sang to her mirror reflection.

> *Winter night, I yearn for the road that leads to the distant past.*
> *Winter night, I dream a dream of a loving family.*
> *Winter night, I drift through the wind and dust of a foreign land.*
> *Is there someone wandering on a winter night without a home?*[9]

Three

Sacrifices

ON THE EVE of the Year of the Rooster of 1981, everyone was on the road. The living visited gravesites to converse with the dead, and the dead returned to places where they could commune with the living. The sky blue Vanagon, traveling north on Route 14, jostled heavy night traffic. Squinty, the driver, reassured the group that he could navigate the old Ho Chi Minh Trail blindfolded, having marched south during wartime. Beside him, One Arm, the mechanic, picked at the festering hole in his chest and worried about unexploded ordnance until Hai asked, "Why care? We're already dead."

The woman had drowned in the South China Sea, and Hai in moonshine. Phuong died of a head injury after jumping off a moving train en route to prison, Squinty and One Arm in war, and Slit-throat, the rooster, on a sacrificial platter for his human ancestors.

The woman did not hesitate when the boys offered to accompany her to the Central Highlands. One Arm fixed her husband's Vanagon and gave it a fresh coat of paint. Squinty proposed taking the mountainous Ho Chi Minh Trail rather than the coastal Highway 1. Hai, paralyzed since birth, wanted to go for a ride. "Free and easy wandering," he said and invited Phuong to come along. The rooster, who had not left the woman's side since she returned from the failed sea escape, stowed away in the van among the transported odds and ends: bottles and jars of seeds and cuttings, a barrel filled with water from the man-made pond and fish swimming in circles under lily pads, and a Phoenix Salon hairstyling kit.

Traveling on Route 14, the van would pass the new economic zone where the woman had spent the last years of her life. She no longer felt fear or sadness, now understanding the freedom she had experienced while imprisoned. All her desires for all that was life had dissipated the moment she had let go.

"No blood pudding?" Squinty asked.

The rooster eyed Squinty and then One Arm, following the conversation.

"We skip the blood pudding," One Arm said. "We can boil the innards for rice gruel and shred the meat for chicken salad."

"The rooster had been sacrificed," Phuong said. "We can't offer our ancestors the same rooster twice."

"We are the ancestors!" Hai exclaimed. "The living make us the offering." He turned to his sister-in-law, who had stayed quiet while they debated preparing chicken as the main dish. "Wasn't that what you'd said? The living should buy flowers for the dead. We're now the rightful receivers of the living's sacrifices."

Camel, Seven Styles

FROM THE BE River, Maia and Na returned to Ho Chi Minh City, where Na said the Maos usually spent their weekends. As they neared Ox Alley, the two women could hear what sounded like the monotonous knocking of a wooden gong. They saw smoke and smelled barbecue and a whiff of blood and rotting meat.

"Charlee Camel," Na said matter-of-factly.

Maia maneuvered the Minsk through the narrow maze of the alleyway to the Winter Night Café. At the gate, they met JP, bleary-eyed with a hangover on a Sunday morning, and No-No, slinking through the *Ochna integerrima* hedge meowing oddly. The orange stray had grown lanky in the days they were away.

JP hugged Na, hesitated, and then awkwardly shook Maia's hand. He updated them on what had happened following Charlee's death on the very morning Maia and Na left the Mekong Delta. He had recorded and sketched the string of events in minute detail in his travelogue. The camel's death had altered the travelers' route. Instead of continuing to the southernmost tip of Vietnam and sailing across the Indian Ocean to Africa, they decided to travel overland, taking the northbound train from Ho Chi Minh City.

"I love trains," Na said. "Where are they going?"

"What are they looking for?" Maia asked.

JP shrugged. "Before traveling to the city, the fruit boy carved the camel with a single cut. He knew exactly where the joints were, and his knife slithered along the seams." JP vigorously sliced the thin air between them with an imagined butcher knife to punctuate his story.

The outdoor café had been transformed into a scene of gong tapping and incense burning, sedating everyone except No-No, who prowled the garden, investigating the division of labor. Not only Uncle Mao, but also the entire Mekong cast, plus the extras from Ox Alley, were there. Mama Mao, Auntie Mao, and the neighborhood women clustered near the well by the guava tree. Uncle Mao, Xuan, and the Public Security Trio assembled beside the man-made fishpond. Under the starfruit tree, the travelers set their wooden crate, pitched their motley tents, and built a hearty campfire.

JP led them to the fire, where the man with the carved serpent staff poured Maia and Na steaming cups of dark lumpy tea.

Remembering Charlee towing her grandmother's hearse upstream, Maia wanted to express her sympathy, but the man hushed her.

"The camel no longer carries the burden." He swung his walking stick to and fro and tapped the ground, raising a cloud of dust to attract No-No's attention. The man watched intently as the orange kitten leaped upon the serpent's tail and growled from deep within.

"What are you looking for?" Maia asked.

The man eyed her. "Mirrors for my teaching of the eternal return."

"What does that mean?"

"To affirm life in all its spectacles, to shout at the end, *da capo*!"

"How do you do that?"

"Self-creation! Compose life, guess its riddles, and re-deem its coincidences." He searched her face. "Is your mir-ror clear and smooth?"[10]

Just then the fruit boy appeared before them. He twirled the stolen rearview mirror from Xuan's red Honda Dream. Light reflected from the campfire.

"No, no. Not that shifty child." The man squinted as if distracted by the glare.

JP whispered in Maia's ear, "Maybe Old Seeker is not seeking anything but himself."

Na walked up to the water-damaged crate. "Who'll cart the box, then? What's in it?" She snapped off a piece of decayed wood and peeked inside. "It's empty!" No-No followed, sniffed, and poked a paw between the crack.

"I'm told it's a stolen spirit from Bangalang," JP said. "You communicate with spirits, don't you?"

"Only if they want to talk. Maia carries her father's ashes. I see him—a big black man."

"Big Al from Love City who works in passport?"

Maia left the bantering between JP and Na to look for her Uncle Mao. When she passed the group of women sitting on their haunches around the well, she heard someone call out, "Our helper!"

Mama Mao motioned Maia to join them among the baskets of foodstuffs, spread out as if the vendors from the market had gathered at the café to sell their produce. There were baskets of lotus seeds, leaves, and roots, sacks of lily bulbs, chrysanthemums, and dandelions, boxes of black and white fungus, jars of dried figs and red dates, and some vessels of strange ingredients that Maia did not recognize.

Mama Mao handed her a large bamboo sieve of fresh mixed herbs and asked, "Con còn biết lặt rau không?"

Sitting down with the women, Maia realized what sounded like the tapping of a wooden gong from afar was Auntie Mao pounding a pestle into a mortar. She had not looked up but continued to smash the mixture of spices, turning it into a saffron pulp that hinted at cinnamon, cardamom, nutmeg, and cloves.

"Camel, seven styles!" Mama Mao announced and then listed the seven dishes:

wolfberry, lily bulb, and fungus salad with camel for sleepless nights
for strength, five-element soup of eye, ear, tongue, tail, and hoof
chrysanthemums and camel blood pudding feed the yin
camel stewed with lily flowers and cloud ears feed the yang
eight treasures of camel in lotus leaves rid toxins
tuckahoe with camel dumplings calm the mind
glutinous rice wine and camel balls bring unity

Mama Mao concluded, "The seven courses will regulate the Qi: clear fire, invigorate blood, brighten eyes, soften hardness, dispel wind, and promote elimination."

Mama Mao chanted the dishes and their functions, and Auntie Mao pounded out her hypnotic rhythm. When Mama Mao fell into a meditative silence, the pestle and mortar beat continued.

"How did you meet Uncle Mao?" Maia asked Auntie Mao.

Her aunt kept pounding the pestle into mortar.

Beside the man-dug fishpond, Uncle Mao, Xuan, and the Public Security Trio sat on low wooden stools and plucked hair off the camel hide spread out on the ground. The five men drank, smoked, and argued about the contents of the mysterious crate.

"Smugglers and contrabands," Comrade Ty said. The Public Security Trio made up their minds and urged Chief Mao to confiscate the box and escort the foreigners from the country.

"You *knew* my mother." Maia interrupted the debate.

Uncle Mao looked up from the putrid camel hide. "You're almost the exact replica of her."

Xuan and the Public Security Trio stopped plucking. The pestle and mortar sound continued, filling the silence.

"Your mother was well taken care of," Uncle Mao said. "But she couldn't wait. I would've taken care of her."

"Like the birds?" she asked.

Xuan recited a parable he had heard:

> *The marsh pheasant has to take ten steps for a peck of food*
> *and a hundred steps for a drink,*
> *but it does not want to be fed in a cage.*
> *Although it might live well in a cage,*
> *it would not wish to be confined.*[11]

Uncle Mao's face was expressionless. "After liberation in 1975, we had the responsibility to rebuild our country. Your mother wished she'd been born earlier or later, but she was caught in between. We met when she was only a few years older than you are now." He paused and studied Maia as if weighing whether he should say more.

She stood her ground.

"She suspected the boat with the men wouldn't sail out to sea," he said. "And it didn't. Anyone who didn't escape was captured and interned in Song Be."

"There's no prison somewhere before the Be River empties into Lake Waterfall Dreams," Maia said, repeating Auntie Mao's vague direction. She felt the men's stares. She suppressed the turmoil of emotions that rose from each new detail of her mother's life. She observed the man before her—Uncle Mao, Chief Public Security Mao, and Warden Mao—all the same man. She knew she would have to sift through his story, but for that moment, she listened.

"I helped her in prison," he said. "I helped her after she was out. I arranged her passage to Vung Tau because that was her last wish."

Ox Pagoda

EN ROUTE TO Vung Tau, Xuan informed the group that they would make a quick stop at Ox Pagoda, where Uncle Mao said Maia's mother often visited. When the white Lada Samara, borrowed from Uncle Mao for the trip, arrived at the pagoda's gate, street hawkers crowded around the car and peered through its open windows at the curious group: Xuan at the steering wheel, Maia in the front passenger seat, and JP, Na, and No-No in the backseat. The tawny kitten wore a fresh camel leather harness attached to a leash looped around Na's wrist.

"Ồ, sư tử con!" exclaimed the bird merchant. The street vendors were more interested in the tethered lion-like cub than selling their carved oxen, caged birds, joss papers and sticks.

"Where are you from?" the fruit lady asked in English.

"Ở đây chứ ở đâu." Na's clear Saigonese accent startled the vendors, who proceeded to hawk their goods.

"Five fruits for the altar."

"Paper money for the afterlife."

"Birds to free your karma."

"Wooden oxen to transport the dead."

On the pagoda's wide steps, Xuan spoke privately with a woman and then deposited a sum in the contribution box. The woman directed them to leave their footwear and belongings outside before entering the softly illuminated inside.

Smoke from incense hung from the ceiling descended the narrow hall in preparation for the morning ceremony. Barefoot women in white garb bore offerings of fruits and glutinous rice for the altar that stood before a calligraphic mural depicting ox herding in an open field. The women met the visitors' eyes briefly, then lowered their heads and stepped around them.

When the metal gong was struck, saffron-robed nuns filed in. The visitors and the tethered creature were guided to the front and told to kneel before the altar. JP on his knees stared straight ahead. He wore the beige khaki pants and now-wrinkled white dress shirt he'd had on the first time they met at the airport. He had not dressed formally since, until today. Na wore a traditional loose-fitting Vietnamese outfit, her hair gathered in a thick braid. Xuan appeared more solemn than usual. Something about her three companions made Maia uneasy. She sensed they had agreed on a plan in which she was the focus yet had no say in the decision.

The plump aging abbess settled into a lotus position next to the altar, and an elder nun knelt beside Maia. More people shuffled in. From the corner of her eye, Maia saw the Public Security Trio kowtowing in unison in a row directly behind her. The echoes of the gong faded, and everyone was in place.

For the next hour, the abbess recited rambling incantations. The monotonous light tapping of the wooden fish-shaped gong lulled Maia into a sleepy trance. Every few minutes, the giant round metal gong was struck with the heavy padded mallet, and the nun prompted her to clasp her palms and bow three times. The abbess's chanting, the reverberations of wooden and metal gongs, and the whispering rustle of their obeisance filled the smoky altar hall.

Maia looked around at the vibrant walls and columns of the pagoda, adorned with dragons, phoenixes, turtles, and unicorns. From her folklore reading, she remembered that the dragon stood for strength, the phoenix for peace, the turtle for longevity, and the unicorn for wisdom. The painted animals stared back at her with steady gazes. *Strength, peace, longevity, and wisdom: are these my desires for myself and for others?* The metal gong sounded again and the nun tapped her to bow.

The morning ceremony ended, the smoke dissipated, and a fragrance of jasmine permeated the air. The elderly nun whispered, "Come with me." She led Maia through the dimly lit pagoda to the sunny backyard, where a calf was grazing beside a dilapidated brick well. The nun nudged the young animal toward the dirt path leading to a field overgrown with vegetation.

"Your mother often spoke of your father."

"You met my parents?"

"Only your mother."

The calf wandered off to forage under the shade of a blossoming flame tree. Its tail swung and swatted at the flies on its back.

"She often said she loved your father not for wealth, status, or fame but for his wish to protect others. He wasn't always successful." The nun smiled ruefully. "Those were her exact words. But during the war, his men trusted he'd keep them alive. Their motto was 'locate and evade.'"

Maia's head spun with confusion. She tried to make sense of what the nun said. The expatriates' homage in America rang hollow in her ears. *Your father fought with courage against the Communists. For his service and sacrifice, he will be remembered.*

Who was she to believe?

The overseas tribute was a star that guided her, a shining light on a single course of action. Its brightness now turned gray. Shadows obscured her path.

"We had family on both sides," the nun explained.

After a long pause, she changed the subject. "I read your mother's oracle ten years ago."

"What did the oracle say?"

"It was over ten years ago, and it was for your mother, but for you—"

I don't believe in prophecy! Maia thought but stopped herself from blurting out the words. She wanted to hear what the nun had to say. What she had just learned about her father lodged in her heart; she needed to sort it out in her head. She watched the calf, roaming from the flame tree toward the stream, shaded by willows under which Xuan and the Public Security Trio stood smoking.

"For you," the nun warned, "there's trouble at the beginning, but the confusion will clear up, and all things will breathe freely again. You must choose your helpers wisely."

Helping Hands Ranch

SMOKING UNFILTERED CAMELS triggered a yearning in Kai that lingered long after the last cigarette. Whether a yearning for someone he had lost or something he never had, he could not say.

"How was I found?" he asked Lee yet again.

"I found you curled up in the ruins of a burning village," Lee repeated. "I dropped the things I carried, placed you in my duffle bag, and walked away."

"Westward?"

"Along a great winding river with many tributaries."

Kai confided in Vinnie, and they set out before daybreak with two gourds of moonshine they promised Cook Cu they would barter. They traveled eastward. When they came to a great river that bent northward, they followed it into the Central Highlands.

"We crossed the border!" Vinnie picked up the pace.

"It's still one jungle." Kai trailed behind, clearing the underbrush with his machete and marking the path for their return.

They walked uphill along the watercourse through the evergreen forest without seeing another human. Clouds floated through treetops like filmy white cloths. In the late afternoon, they reached a savanna-like plateau and came upon a clearing. The clouds were now at their feet. The barren area was cultivated but not fenced in. Undeveloped fruit trees, bushes, and vines formed a perimeter. Wildflowers, medicinal herbs, and root vegetables grew in a field adjacent to the river. They picked and ate red berries from a vine they did not recognize. They washed their faces and drank the cool water. They heard birds and a distinct high-pitched whistling beyond the field.

"Wild dogs on the hunt," Kai said.

The boys trotted upstream toward the whistling. Where the river widened into a lake surrounded by flat boulders and young pines, they saw a group of scantily clad children. The children were washing their clothes on the boulders. Some were cleaning vegetables, and others were fishing with bamboo poles and nets, all the while twittering like birds.

Kai and Vinnie hid behind the pines. When an elfin girl passed near them, they could almost touch her long flowing hair. She smelled of pomelo flowers and sandalwood. Kai sucked in his breath and Vinnie slipped out a low wolf whistle. The girl turned. They ducked behind the pines but continued to watch through the gaps.

"Sweet Jesus," Vinnie breathed.

When the girl took several steps in their direction, the boys froze. Her downcast gaze made her look as if she were sleeping. She tilted her head, turned an ear toward them, and listened for a moment before rejoining the children.

"Vin, she didn't see us, did she?"

"No. Sleeping Beauty can't see with them eyes."

They watched the children from behind the pines. As the sun crimsoned in the western sky, the children left the lake, chirping like a flock of birds. Some dragged themselves over the ground, others helped a few along, and the rest carried baskets of the things washed or caught in the water. They traveled close to the riverside with the girl at the lead, now and then whistling.

"Wild dogs?" Vinnie looked at Kai.

"That's the whistling of a wild dog."

Leaving the shore, the children continued through the pine forest.

"Let's see where they're going," Kai said.

"No."

"Why not?"

"Something's in the water . . . in the soil." Vinnie's voice was quiet. He suddenly stuck a finger down his throat and forced himself to gag. His stomach convulsed violently for what seemed like a long time until he threw up a foamy red berry mush. Wiping his mouth, he said weakly, "Let's get back."

"No," Kai said.

"You're one of them, aren't you?"

"What?"

"You're one of them," Vinnie said again. "That night I shot into the bush, everyone thought I was trigger-happy, but when I saw you, I thought I saw a . . . a . . . I don't know what I saw. Let's go."

Kai seemed not to hear.

Night came.

They followed the flickering yellow light in the direction the children had disappeared. They cut through the dark forest, crossed a hilly open field, and entered a young bamboo grove. They found a footpath leading to a fence and a thatched longhouse with square windows through which the light shone.

"Wait here," Kai said.

Before Vinnie could stop him, Kai jumped the fence and vanished into the stretch of darkness with a gourd of moonshine. Appearing outside a lit window, Kai paused and then slipped through the bright light. Vinnie watched for movements and listened for a commotion inside the house but only became more aware of the wind rustling through the pine forest, the river rushing over stones, and nocturnal animals grunting in the distance.

He was startled by a sudden burst of sounds in unison, followed by back and forth calls from different directions. He could not tell whether they were human or animal. He thought they came from inside the shelter. He waited, enclosed in the night. He wanted to make a run for the square of light but froze when he heard hissing near his ear. Trembling, he slowly turned toward the sinister sound.

Kai was standing beside him, grinning like an imp and shaking a bamboo tube filled with sand. "I traded the moonshine!"

When they trekked back to the campground under the starlit sky, Kai asked Vinnie why he had called the girl Sleeping Beauty.

"If a true love kissed her, she'd wake up, and they'd live happily ever after." Vinnie looked at Kai. "Are you true love?"

They did not talk about their outing again until Lee pressed them.

"It's like a ranch in the middle of nowhere with only children," Vinnie reported. "Kai snuck through the window and stole their serpent."

"I *traded* the moonshine." Kai shook the brightly painted bamboo tube he had been carrying around camp. Vinnie thought it sounded like a hissing serpent from the abyss; for Kai, the sound of sand in the bamboo echoed like falling rain and rejuvenated his spirit.

"What did you see?" Lee asked. "Did anyone see you?"

"There was a woman without hair like Cook Cu, and all the children were—"

"Not normal," Vinnie said.

"They helped one another," Kai said. "The right hand helped the left."

"You could be a ranch hand." Vinnie peered at Kai. "Twittering and charred-face, you'd fit right in at the Helping Hands Ranch."

Lee was of the same mind with Vinnie that the boys should not eat, drink, or swim in the water, no matter how hungry, thirsty, or hot they were. He made them promise to observe only from afar. Vinnie suspected something was in the water and soil, but Lee was certain the area was poisoned, recalling the nightmarish rain from the C-123s that turned the forest a sick yellow. He could not convince the boys not to go back to the lake, nor could he bring himself to cross the border with them. He had taught Kai all he could about surviving the jungle. There seemed nothing more he could do. *Sho ga nai*, his father would have said.

Each time the boys returned, Lee would sigh with relief. He listened to the tunes of nature they picked up from the children: the shrill cries of the black-shanked douc, the songs of the golden-winged laughingthrush, the hiss of the water monitor, and the rustling wind through a young pine forest. He listened in anticipation of a sea change.

The Bay of Boats

ONCE CALLED CAP Saint Jacques, a seaport for trading ships from Europe, Vung Tau today drew local vacationers, searching for shade under pines or anchoring their umbrellas in the sand and stretching out beneath to catch the breeze. The hotels, motels, and inns were all full, but Uncle Mao had a comrade in the National Oil Company whose villa on the front beach was vacant.

Soft morning rays reflected off the water and pale sand. From the villa's terrace, Maia could see JP and Na bobbing in the waves and hear their laughter. The lightness of their play distracted her until a group of barefoot women meandering along the shore came into view. The women bore large woven bamboo baskets and wore loose black bottoms and áo bà ba tops, their faces hidden under cone hats.

"People came here to cross the sea," Xuan said, leaning against the balustrade, "to Hong Kong, the Philippines, Indonesia, Malaysia." He looked at her. "Your mother came here to leave the country—"

"For a life elsewhere."

He lit a cigarette. "Mai," he called her name softly, "if you haven't heard from your Má after all these years . . ."

She slipped off her sandals, hooked her fingers through the straps, and stepped off the terrace onto the sand. The beach was silky and cool. She then felt the sharp broken shells beneath her bare feet and wanted to put her sandals back on. She kept walking. She did not want to hear his words. She knew he could not let go of his own past, nor could she stop searching without knowing what happened.

The women were gathering shellfish. Every summer, they came from nearby villages with their young children and old parents. They stayed in makeshifts along the back beach, away from the tourists. They did not know much about the Bay of Boats, except that on certain days in certain spots, they could find clams in abundance. They had never met a grown person looking for her mother.

"She left because she knew you could feed yourself."

Someone tossed a spade on the sand near Maia.

"My child is sick today. Mr. Sky sends you to help."

The women beckoned Maia to come closer and showed her the tiny holes in the sand where water was squirting up. "Dig here."

Maia worked alongside the clam pickers. She followed them from one cluster of holes to the next, from the front beach, around Nghinh Phong Point, to the back beach. After hours of bending and digging, her body stiffened and she felt lightheaded from dehydration. She wanted shade and water, but she continued until they stood before the shanties. Erected along the mossy stone wall that separated the boulevard from the sandy shore, the makeshifts were invisible from afar. The low roofs were made from bits and pieces of black moldy tin. The cardboard sides were the color of sand, making the shelters undetectable to those not looking.

The women set the baskets among their scanty belongings and poured Maia a small tin of warm pandan tea. She asked for a second cup and a third. They disappeared into the shanties, leaving her with an old woman and a sallow-skinned girl who were tending several cooking fires. Over one was a large pot of rice mixed with barley. The second cooked cassava. The smallest boiled an earthy mixture of dried barks, leaves, and berries.

"What's the brew for?" Maia asked.

"A concoction from the Isle Pagoda," the old woman said. The morning before, when it was low tide, she had walked a third of a kilometer to the isle off the southwest coast. The nuns there grew varieties of medicinal plants.

"For the girl?"

"No. For her father, my son-in-law." The old woman glared at the man swinging in a hammock nearby. He was badly sunburnt and unshaven and had a distended potbelly. His dull eyes stared blankly before him. "He hasn't slept for days. Can't sleep. Can't eat. Can't work. The brew will help."

The Sea Swift

"FRESH CATCH FROM the sea! Fresh catch from the sea!"

The cry from outside the shanty woke Maia. The clam diggers had gone for the morning, and the old woman and young girl were nowhere in sight. Only the potbelly man was left sleeping in the hammock, the wind rocking him to and fro, lulling him into deeper oblivion.

Shoppers gathered near the water's edge, picking over live fish on a plastic mat on the sand. A boy about seven or eight years old was culling small silvery fish, gray crabs, and prawns into a red plastic pail. When he saw Maia, he called out, "Cá tươi! Cá tươi!"

After people left with their purchases, Maia bought the rest for ten thousand đồng and walked back to the shanties with the fish. The man was still lying in the exact position in the hammock. When she came to wake him, it occurred to her that he might not be sleeping. Her heart began to pound.

"The brew will help," his mother-in-law had said.

Maia quickly put the fish in a pail of water and placed it near the blackened sand where the cooking fires had burned. As she turned to leave, she saw the boy and a wiry man, an older replica of the boy, watching her from several yards away. The fisherman glanced past her at the shanties, the sleeping man, and the pail of fish. He then picked up the plastic mat, shook the water and sand from it, and folded it into quarters. He tucked the folded mat under his arm. The boy was at his side with two large woven baskets.

"Looking for work?" the man asked Maia. "Come with us."

He started off toward the shore with his son dragging the large baskets, making winding parallel lines in the sand. "See that boat?" the man called back, pointing to a pink wooden vessel bobbing in the distance. "That's the *Sea Swift*. We built her. She can take us to Hong Kong, the Philippines, Indonesia, Malaysia, anywhere!"

"How do you get there?" Maia followed. She slipped off her sandals at the water's edge, where the broken shells had been smoothed by the waves.

"To Hong Kong, the Philippines, Indonesia, or Malaysia?"

"No. How do you get to that pink boat?"

His young son pushed the baskets into the water and climbed into one while keeping a hand on the other.

"You can ride with the boy," the man said. "We'll go around Nghinh Phong Point back to Ben Sao Mai. You can get off at the front beach."

"Wait! Could you help me—?"

The man had climbed into the other basket, his hands sculling water to keep from drifting away, but she could not finish her question. Instead, she waded into the deep. "You'll let me off at the front beach?"

The father and son nodded, their baskets bobbing up and over the incoming waves.

The basket tossed erratically when she climbed in with the boy, who squatted on one side. Between them was the red plastic pail with the miscellaneous fish, crabs, and prawns.

"Be still and balance yourself," the man called across the waves.

Glancing back, she could barely make out the tin-roof shanties along the dark stonewall or the man in the hammock, knocked out, she now realized, by a sleeping potion from the Isle Pagoda. She hoped the concoction would wear off before the fish spoiled in the heat.

The *Sea Swift* was a twenty-foot fishing boat built from young poplar wood. The deck did not have much walking space. Its sides were lined with barrels of fresh water, more barrels for fish, and several plastic containers of gasoline. There were cooking pots and a gasoline stove in one corner of the deck, a heap of fishing nets in another, a narrow plank bed inside the cabin, and an oil lamp hanging from the ceiling.

"If the weather is good, we can stay out for days," the man said. "We have enough rice and fuel for two weeks." He started the engine, turning the boat southward along the back beach. The *Sea Swift* glided quietly and smoothly over the waves through the narrow strip of water between the coast and the Isle Pagoda.

"Is fishing your livelihood?" she asked.

"It was my grandfather's, father's, mine, and will be my son's." He gazed at the boy, who was rinsing their small catch in the pail. "Clean them well," he instructed. "Maybe our guest will join us for a meal."

She accepted the invitation.

"Ben Sao Mai in the northwest where I grew up is the oldest fishing district," the man said. "Everybody I know fishes, sells fish, or makes fish soup."

The man steered the vessel around Mui Nghinh Phong, the southernmost tip of Vung Tau. They sailed silently with the rise and fall of the waves in open water. The rough back and forth tossing of the small boat unsettled her. She locked her knees to steady her wobbly legs, but standing stiffly, she was knocked off balance. She gripped the side of the boat, her fingers slipped, and she fell backward onto the deck. The moving sea and shifting sky made her sick to her stomach.

"You don't sail much, do you?" the fisherman asked.

His son peered down at her.

"The last time . . . I was on a boat . . . was long ago."

"Breathe! Breathe! Breathe!" the boy instructed, inhaling and exhaling vigorously. He spread her arms and legs straight out in a corpse pose.

"Relax." The fisherman's voice sounded far away. "Yield. Don't fight it."

She let herself move with the rocking of the deck. She closed her eyes and her breathing slowed, falling into rhythm with the sea. As her body sank deeper into the ocean, she glimpsed a disorienting boundlessness. She bolted upright to keep from falling. She pushed herself to sit up against the side of the boat.

"You're seasick."

She smiled apologetically at the fisherman and his son.

"Are you hungry?"

She nodded.

"It's fish stew today," the boy said. He had cooked the bony fish in thick soy sauce and black pepper, sautéed the tiny crabs and prawns with garlic and sea salt, boiled some greens, and made a pot of rice. There was also tea in a clay kettle.

"You'll feel better with a little food in you." The fisherman turned off the engine. "Then we'll drop you off at the front beach."

He spread a bamboo mat in the middle of the deck, on which the boy placed a large round aluminum tray. They sat cross-legged around their lunch. The boy scooped rice into a ceramic bowl and handed it to her with both hands. The man divided a fish in half with his chopsticks and placed the head portion in her bowl and the tail in his son's. "Let's eat!"

They ate slowly and silently.

"I'm looking for my mother," she finally said out loud. "She came here over ten years ago but no one has heard from her." She swallowed a mouthful of rice to keep a lump from rising in her throat.

The boy moved an empty dish near her. "You can put the fish bones here."

They continued to eat in silence.

When the meal was over, the boy cleared the tray. The man started the engine again. "See that?" He pointed to a massive white statue atop a green peak. "That's Jesus Christ outstretching his arms. I was eighteen when the Americans erected Jesus on that mountain. We knew the South was losing when the high-ranking leaders left the country with their families and relatives. They feared a bloodbath. But my parents believed that Northerners and Southerners were one people."

His face was a tanned leathery mask, wrinkled around the eyes from squinting in the sun. She listened for his allegiance to one side or to the other, but he spoke without emotion.

"From here," he said, "the *Sea Swift* can sail north to Hong Kong, east to the Philippines, or south to Indonesia and Malaysia. We've gone as far as the Con Dao archipelago, where there are plenty of big fish. Beyond the archipelago, there's a small isle where swallows make their nests and lay their eggs. When the morning sun's glowing red, the swallows masquerade in their pink plumage and skip across the sky in a dance with their water reflections."

They sailed past the front beach, the tourist district of luxury hotels, giant colorful umbrellas, and a floating restaurant.

"There's an old man in our neighborhood who captained three boats across the South China Sea," the man said. "Old Man Giac might know something."

Ben Sao Mai, a strip of land between the shore and the foot of Big Mountain, had a heavy fish smell. The neighborhood consisted of some twenty shacks of fishermen and their families, clustering the main paved road that curved around the northwestern coast of Vung Tau. The street was lined with rows and rows of fish and squids and octopuses laid flat on the ground to dry in the sun, like an open market display of motley sandals, flip-flops, and slippers. Where there was no space, the catches were hooked through their heads or mouths and hung vertically on metal racks like enormous earrings from the sea.

Maia followed the fisherman and his son through a wet alley strewn with fish carcasses of guts, fins, scales, and tails. In the backyard of a thatched hut overlooking the shore, they found a man drinking rice whiskey from a gourd and playing chess by himself. He was shirtless, wearing only a pair of loose black pants. His wiry sunburnt back curved over the wooden chessboard. His forehead was creased in deep concentration, his thumb and forefinger holding a chess piece in midair. With his other hand, he grabbed the jug and took a long swig before placing the piece down with an audible click. "Chiếu tướng!" The old man's lips trembled with pleasure.

The fisherman told Maia that Old Man Giac was the most daring in his youth. He went the farthest in the worst weather to catch the biggest fish. He knew the shortest and fastest passage across the South China Sea to Hong Kong, the Philippines, Indonesia, and Malaysia. He made three crossings. On his third trip, he sold his home and took his wife, three sons, and four daughters. He then returned alone. No one knew why he returned. He had never set foot off land again.

Maia approached Old Man Giac. "Mister, my mother came here to escape the country."

The old man's expression changed from contentment to hostility. He brought the jug up to his mouth, tilted his head back, and gulped noisily. He placed the jug down and rearranged the chess pieces on the board, making loud angry click-clack sounds.

"Uncle," the fisherman said, "please help if you can."

Old Man Giac stopped chewing a dried octopus tentacle and looked at Maia with bloodshot eyes, his lips quivering. "If you haven't found your mother," he said, "she's not here but gone to sea."

"What do you mean?"

He studied the chessboard. His forehead wrinkled in concentration.

She reached over and pushed a red soldier one point forward. "Is she living somewhere? Like your wife and children?"

He moved the black chariot. He drank the last drop from the jug. "All gone," he mumbled. "No more."

From Ben Sao Mai, Maia walked eastward along Nguyen An Ninh Street, turning right on Binh Gia, which changed into Xo Viet Nghe Tinh, where she passed the open marketplace, hotels, and massage parlors. Instead of continuing on to the front beach villa, she ducked into the House of Night Water.

Girls in white satin robes clustered around her when she asked for a massage.

"A massage?" they repeated.

"This is a massage parlor, isn't it?"

"Are you with the công an?"

She shook her head, following their gazes through the darkened glass to the Public Security Trio standing outside under the yellow streetlight.

"What kind of massage?" the girl eating a green guava asked. "Do you want a *masseur*?" Before Maia could respond, the girl called out, "Tèo ơi, có khách!"

In came a slim, well-manicured man. He slinked up to Maia and circled her, smelling of musk and vanilla. He jutted his face into her neck and inhaled. "Oh my!" He breathed. "You can use a bath."

The girls looked at one another.

"Đào," the one with the guava called, "bring a bar stool to the backroom." She set aside the half-eaten fruit, introduced herself as Ái, and led Maia to the girls' shared quarters. Đào had stripped to her peach bra and panties and placed a tall stool under the showerhead.

"Everything off," Ái ordered. She disrobed herself and stepped into the shower in crimson lacy undergarments.

Maia's feet dangled above the tile floor when she mounted the stool. Cold water and sharp fingernails made her tremble.

"Just got dumped?" Đào asked.

Ái whispered, "Maybe she's never been in love."

"Why be sad?" Đào said. "Many fish are in the sea. We'll lovelify you to catch another."

The girls cleaned her every fold and indentation. They washed behind her ears, under her arms, between her legs. They tickled the sand from her navel.

Ái shampooed her hair and Đào soaped her body. They used the balls of their fingers to lather up the foams and their sharp nails to scrub off the dead skin. The water cleaned the stickiness of the sand, the crusty salt, and the deep briny smells of the ocean.

They dried her and led her to a twin-sized bed with a white sheet. They bade her to lie down and rubbed her with coconut oil infused with flowers and fruits.

"Fragrant, sweet and tart like a passion fruit," Ái chanted.

Đào caressed her body and studied her face. "You're not bad looking . . . some might find you lovely—" She paused. "You're crying. Why?"

Maia returned to the villa on the front beach to find Na, JP, and Xuan playing chess in the common area.

JP kissed her cheek. "Hmmm," he murmured. "Salty."

Alone in the room, she ran a wide-tooth comb through her still damp hair. Hollow eyes stared back from her dark reflection. She turned from the mirror.

Water Spirits

MAIA STOOD ON a cliff overlooking the southeastern coastline. She waited for a boat to take her to scatter her father's ashes where she believed her mother was at last free.

Na and Xuan remained a few steps away.

JP was at her side. "I heard you wrote a poem," he said.

"You'll feel better," Na said, "if you speak the words aloud."

No-No bounced back and forth, sniffing the air, making hoarse choking sounds.

A seagull swooped, hovered, and then circled as it rose.

"The drowned become spirits," Xuan said. "Those who yearn for them turn into waterbirds that skip upon the crests."

She felt like a tiny pebble, standing between the sky and sea, lost in the great circle of blue. She felt JP's hand on the small of her back. She spoke, her voice barely audible yet firm and steady above the roaring waves.

> *The sea, the Eastern Sea, has stolen a body.*
> *Hong Kong, Philippines, Malaysia, Indonesia:*
> *somewhere near shore, a woman drowned,*
> *but the shore is waves and sand*
> *like the shore of the North Atlantic,*
> *where coconuts grow in a glass.*
> *She's there—waiting.*
>
> *Thirteen, thirteen years passed.*
> *I'm on a fishing boat,*
> *fishing the Eastern Sea.*
> *The spirits know where she is.*

I can't see them.
Can you ask them
where she is?

For proper burial, the sea is not earth.
In dreams, we leave to arrive.
I will scatter you,
but I can't find her.
Will you sail back to America?
By the Pacific, I will wait
by the coconuts that grow in a glass.

Four

The Reunification Express

AUGUST REVOLUTION STREET in Ho Chi Minh City was jammed with bicycles, motorcycles, xe lam, and xích lô in the early evening. Maia sat beside the taxi driver in the front seat with her eyes closed, trying to stay calm. The taxi swerved and jerked along, the driver honking the horn intermittently.

"Please hurry!" Na urged from the backseat.

"Không sao, không sao." The driver assured them that they would make it to the Hoa Hung train station before nightfall.

Maia felt Na's hand on her shoulder.

"Don't worry," Na said. "We'll get there."

Maia opened her eyes, not looking at Na, but in her peripheral vision, she saw the pink heart-shaped sunglasses, and her stomach knotted.

They were catching the overnight train to Nha Trang, whose beaches Na had gushed were "most romantic," enticing JP to come along and Na to accompany them. Maia tried not to get sidetracked with her irritation. After all, Na and JP had helped her escape from Xuan and the Public Security Trio in Vung Tau, now more than a hundred kilometers away. But in due time, she would have to lose them too.

JP, in khaki pants and a white *L'amant* T-shirt he bought in Sadec, sprawled out beside Na in the backseat. His dark hair had coppery streaks from the sun. In his lap No-No perched. Except for a swollen piko, which JP now said was an umbilical hernia, the orange cat seemed strong and jaunty—a new bell on his collar, eyes alert, and ears swiveled forward.

Even in the hazy twilight of Saigon evening, Na's neon pink sunglasses were perched on her face, giving her the air of a gypsy, which she was. The glasses annoyed Maia. Tacky, loud, and cheap, she thought. But she saw that Na, who had quit her job at the Winter Night Café, was living the moment.

Na had laughed off JP's suggestion of looking for her biological father in the U.S., laughing off a ticket to America. "Sống bụi đời," she would say of her living as the dust of life. In a country that shunned those of mixed blood, especially the offspring of Vietnamese women and American GIs, Na flaunted her black Amerasian presence and dreamed of one day crooning away whatever woes life brought her.

"I see," JP said but was unconvinced. He muttered to himself, as if quietly turning the phrase *dust of life* over and over in his head, trying to understand her.

Though they seemed opposites, Na and JP had agreed to play the same game with the same rules of full disclosure. In each other's company, they unveiled themselves, yet remained strangers, keeping a certain distance and insisting on their quirks and idiosyncrasies. They became ever more enigmatic, their new selves tantalizing. What puzzled Maia was their sudden silence. They had been full of chatty flirtation since the Winter Night Café, but even their teaching No-No how to meow more melodiously had stopped.

The Hoa Hung train station was almost deserted except for a blue uniformed porter ushering the last passengers onto the *Reunification Express*. Passing through the colossal glass doors and crossing the spacious oil-stained tile floor under high arched ceilings, Maia wondered what the travelers had been like centuries ago. As they hurried aboard, she thought she saw the motley group, hauling the mysterious crate into the cargo compartment.

The train blew its whistle and pulled out of the station. Maia, Na, and JP carrying No-No trailed one another through the rickety corridor, looking for their compartment. They stepped aside for vendors who hustled by with newspapers, water bottles, and hard candies softening in the heat. The vendors headed to an exit. They jumped off before the train accelerated to full speed, leaving Saigon for the South China Sea and then heading northward to the coastal city of Nha Trang.

Na had convinced Maia to change her reservation from a private sleeper to three berths together. The only sleepers available were in a six-bunk compartment. When they stepped through the sliding metal gate into the cramped smoky compartment, the three occupants on the right stack eyed them. The three bunks in the left stack were empty.

"Họ là người gì vậy cô?" a woman in the bottom bunk asked Maia. The woman put her *Kiến Thức* magazine on the wooden table between the two stacks of bunks. The man slouching on the top bunk continued to puff on a cigarette. In the middle berth, an elderly woman curled on her side with motion sickness. Her eyes were also on them.

"Toi la nguoi My," JP answered and climbed onto the top bunk. His atonal Vietnamese "I-am-American" seemed to bewilder them. The curled-up old woman twisted open her vial of dầu xanh and rubbed more green menthol oil across her forehead, under her nostrils, and on her throat.

Na picked the middle bunk and Maia took the bottom. The hard sleeper had a dingy straw mat that did not cushion the wooden plank. The space between the bunks was too narrow for her to sit upright. Lying flat on her back, Maia ate stale bread and drank lukewarm water from a bottle. Above, she could hear JP opening wrappings of crackers. In the middle bunk, Na peeled banana leaves off sticks of nem chua for herself and No-No. Between bites of sour fermented pork with fresh chili pepper and garlic, Na ate raw lotus seeds, shelling them and dropping their round green husks onto the floor with the banana leaves.

The wind howled through windows and down the metal corridor, purging passengers' murmurings and odors from the train. Maia propped her head on her bag and gazed out the window into the openings of brick homes that sprang up along the tracks. From the ceiling of each slant-roof dwelling, a single naked light bulb illuminated the bare knick-knacks of a family. These windowed lives appeared like a slide show, frame after frame with different actors. She ached for the warmth from the glow of homes passing by.

She thought of her childhood. What would have been if they had stayed back with her mother? A girl shoveled dirt to build mud houses. A kid with a tree branch slingshot fired pebbles at toads along the railway. She would have played hide-and-seek and swung from the sung tree. How could she believe that her mother was alive?

When she drifted off to sleep, she dreamed of the sea.

Xuan steps on the crests of waves billowing like white clouds. The dim glow of his lit cigarette flickers like nocturnal insects with the movement of his hand. He comes toward her, calling her. He lights another cigarette, then another. He smokes his hundredth. Hundreds of fireflies flash like the steady glow of a lighthouse beam that steers her to a shore and a woman building sandcastles.

Come, the woman beckons. The wind screeches and roars, and waves crash and pound against the vessel. The woman has scattered the contents of her basket on the white sand—a jar of seahorses, a bottle of ocean water, a pouch of cuttings and seeds.

Shhhhh! Her voice cracks from dehydration. Your father's asleep. She seeds the sand in a crescent moon pattern and plants the cuttings along the wide arc. I'm growing a sea hedge, she says.

When enormous waves threaten the sandcastle, the woman gathers her seahorses and bottled water and puts them into her basket. She reaches to tuck a loose strand of hair behind Maia's ear, cold fingers scratching her cheek like sea coral and wet sand.

The ocean swells up, a huge wave rolls in, sweeps far up the shore, and then recedes, returning the sandcastles and the woman to sea.

When the *Reunification Express* arrived in Nha Trang at dawn, the station was crowded with taxicabs, honda-ôm motorcycles, and xích lô. Haggard, weary old men in rags and flip-flops, cigarettes tucked behind their ears or hung from their dry lips, called out to the passengers as they stepped off the train. "You! You! You! Help an old man make a living." They pedaled their creaky pedicabs and pushed their taxi-motorbikes alongside potential customers.

A young taxicab driver leaned against a sleek silver Toyota. He sported dark slacks, a white dress shirt, and a tie. Na beckoned and he came.

An old man cursed, "Địt mẹ con gái điếm!"

Another jeered, "Cái lồn có vừa con cặc thằng Tây đó không?"

Maia felt her face redden and her heart beat fast. A guidebook advised overseas Vietnamese women traveling with foreigners to speak to the locals in English. She swung around, met the old gazes, and yelled, "You, you low class, provincial, narrow-minded, pathetic, pea-brain dirtbags!" They stared at her. Their faces puckered in puzzlement.

JP looked perplexed. She switched to Vietnamese, "Đồ, đồ—" She broke off. She did not know any cuss words in Vietnamese.

Na smiled at the xích lô pedalers and taxi-motorbike drivers.

In the air-conditioned Toyota, JP asked, "What was that? What just happened?" He, Na, and the cat took the backseat. Maia sat in front with the solemn-faced driver.

"They think she's your girl," Na said.

"Maia." JP tugged at her shirtsleeve. "Is that true?"

She turned to him and translated. "Fuckin' American's whore, your cunt's big enough for the white man's dick?"

JP's face fell, and something flickered in Na's eyes.

Family sundry stores, service shops, and food stalls opened up along the wide boulevards where light morning traffic flowed. Poinciana trees dropped red and yellow butterflies onto the wind. The salty smell of the sea became more noticeable as they came toward Tran Phu Boulevard, where palm trees lined the median. When the glistening white sand and blue waters came into view, Maia tried to push the incident from her memory, but the ragged flip-flop existence of the old men weighed on her mind.

She thought of the world of Suzie Wong, the quiet American's Phuong, and Kim of *Miss Saigon*. Were these women her legacy? Was she another Kim, Phuong, or Suzie?

She breathed in the damp, heavy air and gazed into the distance. She was a swimmer gliding effortlessly beneath the waves, a flying fish leaping above. She was reminded of her dream on the *Reunification Express*. The woman with the red basket haunted her: her cold slender hands, rough with salt crust, her tired eyes, her words, her smell full of the ocean.

I am her daughter, Maia whispered, and aloneness washed over her—powerful, cold, and vast.

Illegitimacy

LEE HAKAKU BOYDEN did not tell his hānai son everything he remembered, and the one detail he kept to himself consumed him. By the time his platoon had arrived on the outskirts of the Central Highlands, the hamlet was already burned to the ground. Many believed it was the People's Army, others blamed the ARVN, and some suspected American soldiers.

After twenty-something years, who was directly responsible seemed to matter less. The aftermath was the same. A village had been reduced to ashes, and no one but Lee heard the crying.

Whenever asked, Lee repeated only the bare bones of what happened next. He found a scorched child curled up in the burning ruins. He dropped the things he carried, secured the child in his duffle bag, and walked away.

He did not regret leaving his platoon. By then, he was convinced of the illegitimacy of war. But what haunted him, the one detail he had not told anyone, was what he saw in the child's grip—a crumbled photograph of Ho Chi Minh, which he pried from the tiny fingers and let drop into the fire along with the things he carried.

The ashes scattered in the wind, but a question remained lodged in Lee's memory and resurfaced in Kai's yearning. Why was Ho in the child's death grip?

Observing the child over the years, Lee felt as if time stood still, and he could only guess his age. It had been more than two decades, yet the child had not grown from his skeletal frame. He suspected the boy might have been older when found, perhaps a severely malnourished teen—stunted and weightless riding in his duffle bag.

Though he had not physically changed, Kai seemed to experience an *increase in being*. Lee was pleased with the child's metamorphosis from a burned block of wood, seemingly oblivious to the world, to a sponge that absorbed all there was around him. From Lee, the boy learned a confluence of people's languages in a contact zone. From the children, he imitated the calls of the mountain. From Cook Cu, he concocted bits and pieces of the jungle for sustenance. From the passersby, he accumulated histories of dispersal: the stateless seeking asylum, the lowlanders crossing the sea, the indigenous forced from the highlands.

Lee was a proud Pops until the boy came under the influence of Vinnie Huynh, who filled his ears with *The Art of War*.

"We must assess the way of the Communist regime, its command and regulation," Vinnie told the group. "We must anticipate our enemy's strengths and weaknesses."

"How do you propose we gain such information?" a man asked.

"Foreknowledge," Vinnie said and then quoted the ancient manual:

> *Such foreknowledge cannot be had from ghosts and spirits,*
> *educed by comparison with past events,*
> *or verified by astrological calculations.*
> *It must come from people—people who know the enemy's situation.*

"And who are these people who know the enemy's situation?"

Vinnie and Kai exchanged furtive glances.

"The two of you?"

The boys nodded in unison, and Vinnie recited another passage from the manual:

> *There are five kinds of spies that can be employed:*
> *local spies, inside agents, double agents,*
> *expendable spies, and unexpendable spies.*
> *When the five kinds of spies are all active,*
> *and no one knows their methods of operation,*
> *this is called the imperceptible web.*[12]

"And the two of you are—?"

"Unexpendable!" Kai could not hold still the rattling of his painted bamboo tube.

"We're cultivating local spies," Vinnie whispered. "We have eyes and ears—"

"You boys are in communication with the highlanders?"

"With the children!"

Kai shook the bamboo, and Vinnie whistled the sound of wind through pine trees. The two echoed the shrilled cries of the black-shanked douc, the songs of the golden-winged laughingthrush, and the hiss of the water monitor.

Lee interrupted the duet. "Weren't you warned to watch only from afar? Have you been seen by the children?"

"Our purpose is to infiltrate."

"Looking like the two of you?" someone asked. "The Lone Ranger and Tonto?"

"Kai blends in," Vinnie said. "He's in love with a girl with long hair that smells like wood and flowers."

"It's just a girl." Kai clasped the rain stick to his chest.

"Not any girl," Vinnie said. "Sleeping Beauty's our eyes and ears."

Lee scrutinized the pair. Vinnie was all talk, and Kai was blushing. Perhaps their excursions beyond the campground's perimeter were nothing more than youthful restlessness. Lee wanted to believe wholeheartedly that Kai's yearning could be assuaged by his love for another—however conflicted or ideal, real-life or fairytale.

Sunrise

Clouds Motel in Nha Trang was a concrete quadrangle. Two rows of single-story rooms faced a rock garden where yellow chrysanthemums grew in oblong planters. Their shared room was painted white and bare of decoration. Three single beds lined side-by-side, perpendicular to the wall. Through two large windows, the breeze swayed white curtains, making them fly like young girls' skirts on a windy day.

White, like an infirmary ward, like mourners at a funeral, like heaven.

But what Maia craved was blank white space. The knots in her stomach had tightened and an ache swelled at the nape of her neck. She felt restless yet weighted down. She thought of shutting her eyes to clear her head before slipping off to the Central Highlands. Twenty minutes to the Liên Tỉnh Express Bus Station. She would take a xích lô. No regular bus schedule. When a bus filled up, it would take off. Phoenix Pass before nightfall.

"I need a nap," she said and settled on the bed beside the windows where No-No was batting at the white curtains.

Na wanted to go for a swim and disappeared into the bathroom to change into her skimpy neon pink bikini. They could hear her humming a song about clouds' illusions.

JP retrieved the tube of sunblock from his pack. He squeezed the lotion into his palm, spread it on both hands, and applied it on his face, neck, chest, and arms. He pulled off his T-shirt. The tattoo on his upper arm was now barely visible under his tan. "Could you put some on my back?" He handed Maia the Hawaiian Tropic and sat at the edge of her bed. The scents of coconut oil, plumeria, and passion fruit filled the room. Under her hands, his muscles felt taut then relaxed. "Hmmm . . . It's the first time you've touched me."

"What?"

"Nothing. Don't stop."

"Now that I've touched you, I have to kill you."

"Okay. Before that—" He unzipped his khaki pants.

"No. Oh no. Wait!"

"I have swim trunks underneath." He lowered his pants. "Come with us for a swim," he said. No-No had stopped clawing the curtains. His nose twitched and wrinkled, sniffing the air. Finding the fragrance on JP, he licked and gnawed him.

"Okay, done."

"I'll put some on you."

"Uh-uh."

"What are you afraid of?" He turned to look at her. "Are you still angry at those old men at the train station?"

The room seemed whiter. The orange fur ball rolled between them, purring and snuffling at the Hawaiian Tropic. She gazed into eyes like clear turquoise waters. Waves undulated, rippling. Their breaths, shallow and warm.

"I'm not afraid," she said and fell back onto the bed, closing her eyes.

"Mai," Na called, coming into the room. "You sick?"

"Shhhhh!" JP hushed. "C'mon, Na."

Footsteps pattered on cement floor. The doorknob turned, the door squeaked open, and then closed. Through the window, she could hear JP's low voice and Na's laughter. The wind blew the scent of suntan lotion from the room.

Voices faded. No-No curled up on the windowsill. She pulled the bleached sheet over her body and curled beneath it, listening to the waves rolling and crashing against the shore. White, like illusions of clouds. She visualized white empty space and saw turquoise waters. She breathed in and out. Her hand reached for the jade locket around her neck. She clicked it open and touched its cool hollow inside.

Off the coast of Vung Tau, she had scattered ashes like sand from her jade locket, gone in the wind over the South China Sea.

But the urn was empty.

Xuan's gaze was steady. "We've placed your father's remains where they belong," he said. His eyes squinted against the wind. He seemed nonchalant.

The small rickety boat sailed past the Con Dao archipelago. The fisherman was relieved not to go farther and turned back toward land.

That last night in Vung Tau, they drank tea with the clam pickers on the back beach. Maia served Xuan and the Public Security Trio hot cups of herbal brew from the nuns on the Isle Pagoda. They needed it, she thought—a deep oblivious sleep.

At daybreak, the four men slept, legs dangling from the hammocks, mouths opened wide and eyes closed shut.

Maia, Na, and JP carrying No-No made their escape.

In the morning grayness, a ball bouncing back and forth woke Maia from a heavy sleep since the afternoon before. The beds had been pushed together under a single mosquito net that billowed like clouds with the sluggish turning of the rattan ceiling fan. Beside her, Na and JP slept, bodies intertwined. Curling at their feet, No-No stirred when Maia left the bed. He yawned and arched his back, all the while watching her change into the yellow đồ bộ. He sidled up to her and circled her legs with his tail. When she gathered him up and pressed her face into his, he wrinkled his nose and pushed all four paws against her. He slipped from her arms and through the window into the gray light.

"Goodbye, Pōpoki."

She collected her things and secured her bag. She glanced at the sleeping forms, still shifting and entangled in each other's dreams. JP's journal lay on the nightstand, a pen wedged midway between the pages. She picked up the journal and moved toward the windows for light, thinking she should leave a note. Instead of writing, she peeked at the entries on the places they had been, curious scribble and unfinished sketches. She was again arriving at the airport at noon, this time from another viewpoint. She was intrigued by the observations of things she had not noticed. Marginal notes on one page and parallel curving lines on the next conjured flickering light in grayness. She saw a figure stoking ashes to find embers.

Outside, a single bouncing ball became many, pulling her attention from JP's travelogue of juxtaposed images and askew details. She peered through the window. The boulevard was packed with people playing soccer, badminton, and đá cầu. The sounds of shuttlecocks rocketing off badminton racquets, soccer balls against bodies, and the calls of celebration mingling with defeat filled the morning. On the sand across the boulevard, a group of women in their sixties and seventies moved their arms and bodies in slow fluid motions, mirroring the continuous extension and retreat of the shoreline. They stood facing the horizon where a bright orange sun beckoned.

Maia replaced her bag under the bed, left the room, and walked past the xích lô parked beside the motel, heeding the pedalers who were still sound asleep in the passenger seats. She crossed the boulevard and stood on the sand under the coconut palms several feet from the women whose movements rose and fell with the ocean waves.

"Thái Cực Quyền," a teenager said, coming up to her. He raised his thin arms exaggeratedly in a Tai Chi pose of a white stork flapping its wings. His grin ended in a yawn. He knotted his tousled hair into a bun, exposing a dent imprinted across his cheek where he had leaned against a bar while sleeping. "Mothers from the North," he explained. "They're looking for their children's remains in the South." He pointed to the group's transportation, a Soviet vehicle with Cyrillic script still detectable under yellow paint. "I pedal xích lô. Need a ride somewhere? A beautiful sunrise from the towers?"

"No."

He chanted a hymn to Mother Earth:

> *Born from the puff in the sky and the fluff in the sea,*
> *Ninety-seven husbands and thirty-nine daughters,*
> *Creator of Earth, trunk of eaglewood, aroma of rice.*[13]

He crossed the street. "Come, before the sun is high!" He disappeared through the crowd and returned minutes later, pushing a rickety beat-up bicycle. "My xích lô needs fixing."

The boy took her on his bicycle down Tran Phu Boulevard along the South China Sea. They turned left on Yersin

Street and then right on April Second. Heading north, they crossed the Cai River. They were strangers though she did not feel strange, sitting close to him on the rear rack, her arms around his thin waist. She could smell the sweat and hear his breathing when the road sloped up. On flat land, he pedaled easily and talked as if they were longtime friends.

Across the Xom Bong Bridge, they arrived at the ancient towers on the hilltop erected by the first people. There had been eight structures, but only four remained. Except for some remnants of old masonry coated under layers of lichen, most of the towers had been rebuilt recently with concrete and red bricks. They climbed atop the boulders behind the four towers and looked down over the bridge. The sun rose higher and painted the thatched huts and fishing boats along the river in an orange light that reflected off the water. As the wind blew, she felt the delicate fabric of her yellow đồ bộ against her skin, and images from JP's travelogue entered her mind. Lines blurred and spaces opened. She stood in the sanctuary of Mother Earth, momentarily transfixed in the morning glow of her childhood home.

Homing

As SOON AS they could fly, her father wanted to release the pair of squabs he had rescued on a gusty rainy night. In the frigid Philadelphia winter, he cracked open the window of their third-floor apartment and shooed the fledglings away, but they always returned. They paced the narrow window ledge, gawked sideways through the pane, and cooed until he let them back in. They were rock doves that flocked the City of Brotherly Love.

Windblown from their nest in the tall steeple of the St. Thomas Aquinas Church, the squabs were a few days old when found. No feathers, only yellow down covered their young awkward bodies. In months, the male grew big with sleek gray feathers, black-checkered wings, and blue iridescence around his neck. The female remained small and dark. The pair had distinct personalities. The male strutted with his puffed-up chest, pecked quick and hard, and cooed thunderously. The female was timid, quiet, and observant of their surroundings. They hung together, preened each other, and nestled on a corner bookshelf at night.

During the day, the birds followed her father everywhere in the rented studio and greeted him at the door when he came home. In the summer months, he opened the window for them to freely fly away and return. The squabs became mama and baba to squabs that left, but Mama Nàng and Baba Chàng stayed. They built many nests in the third-floor home.

The pair seemed as enchanted with reading as her father. Whenever he reclined in bed with a book, the male would perch on his shoulder, the female on his chest. In the morning, the threesome practiced English.

> *Good morning, Chàng!*
> *Coo roo-c'too-coo!*
> *How are you today, Nàng?*
> *Coo roo-c'too-coo!*
> *Today we'll learn the verb to be.*
> *Coo roo-c'too-coo!*

In the afternoon, they peered at the diagrams and instructions in his auto mechanic manuals. Their nights were filled with self-help guides and the world's classics.

Born into the First Indochina War and conscripted into the second, her father longed for a time when he did not fear for his and others' physical survival. With the war seemingly in a distant past, he lost himself in stories that illuminated what life should be. He imagined living as humans should. In the twilight of Philadelphia evenings when he took flight with these ideals, forgetting the heaviness of his body, the rock doves were his companions. In those moments when he believed freedom could be attained in living, he felt at peace.

The pair followed her father and Maia when they moved to another apartment, where there was more space for the used books he accumulated from library giveaways and thrift store sales. Their new place was on the ground floor on which the kitchen opened to the backyard, a narrow concrete enclosure adjacent to an alley where the neighborhood cats roamed. The kitchen door was often left ajar for the birds to come and go freely. In the first week, the male went missing for several days, but he returned. In a letter to Maia's mother, her father wrote that the male got lost and the female led him home.

Soon after that incident, her father found a sleek gray feather on the kitchen floor and suspected the alley cats were on the hunt. He built a makeshift cage out of an old shopping trolley to keep the birds safe at night. The cart was forty-two inches tall, and twenty-four-by-eighteen inches wide, with gaping openings. He ran wires through the openings to narrow the gaps. He removed the two wheels and secured the trolley in a corner of their backyard. Each night before bed, he whispered, "Good night, Little Bird. See you in the morning, Little Bird." He put the pair in their cage.

In hindsight, it was the perfect trap.

One morning, they found only the female and the remains of her mate's feathers.

Operations

XUAN WAS WAITING at Clouds Motel when Maia returned from the sunrise. He leaned against the yellow chrysanthemum planter, his weight on his right side, and his left foot turned slightly in. He was clasping a small brass container close to his body. He shifted when he saw her and limped slowly forward, dragging his left foot. Closer, she saw a muscle quiver at the corner of his left eye.

"Enjoying yourself?" he asked. He held out the brass container, an ancient imperial dragon. "Your father's ashes," he said. "It was placed at Ox Pagoda the morning we made our offerings before Vung Tau. I've retrieved it—a different urn, but your father's ashes."

She did not reach for it.

He continued to hold the dragon in mid-air, fingers gripping its raised camel-like head and curling ribbon tail. "If you wish, we can arrange another sea burial."

She walked past him toward her room.

"Come back to Ho Chi Minh City," Xuan said.

She glanced at the xích lô boy standing by the motel's entrance. He would wait to take her to the Liên Tỉnh Express Bus Station for five thousand đồng.

"The Central Highlands are closed to foreigners," Xuan said quietly, keeping a distance between them.

Out of nowhere, fat Pâté and Cross-eyed Lai reappeared, more robust than she remembered, but there was no sign of Comrade Ty. They flanked her and gripped her arms.

"Get your things. You must come with us."

She tried to wiggle from them, ripping her shirt. They released their grips.

At the doorway, No-No meowed and lashed his tail.

Pâté and Lai paced around the chrysanthemums, the round buttons on their public security uniforms glaring under the sun.

Maia reached down and scratched the cat's damp, sticky hair. Pâté and Lai stopped their pacing. She unlocked the door to an empty room and saw a note on her bed. She recognized the page torn from JP's travel journal. Pâté and Lai were at the door. She slipped the note into her pants pocket.

When the men escorted her from Clouds Motel, the xích lô boy remained in his passenger seat, eyes hooded. A few feet behind, No-No trotted with tail curled upward, sniffing here and there along the path.

The public security station was a redbrick square near the open market. A hushed conversation about her affiliation ensued when they took her in. Xuan ordered the chief công an to lock her up. He limped from the room with the dragon clutched to his chest. Pâté and Lai followed.

"She with the group caught at the border?"

"They're all dead."

"Not all of them."

"Well, this one entered through Tan Son Nhat. Why was she let go?"

"On Tết, a Vietnamese male carrying a U.S. passport was stopped at the airport."

"An IVC member, wasn't he? Whatever happened to him?"

"Shot by a firing squad of seven."

"No, it was lethal injection. Didn't even feel it."

"With the three-drug protocol? Isn't there a shortage with the trade ban?"

"They used domestic poisons."

"Are those reliable?"

"Do you know what's uncostly and unfailing? The guillotine."

"The country would be filled with bloody ghosts demanding their heads. With lethal injection, the dead are pain-free and unmarked. The heart just stops."

The men confiscated her bag and took her to a six-by-ten-foot cell, secured with a rusty padlock and chain. The inside was dark except for holes and slits of sunlight that fell through the cracks. A heavy musty smell of wet earth hung in the air. She groped for the only object against the far wall. The narrow plank bench creaked when she sat down. She saw outlines of passersby and their feet through the gaps in the door and space underneath—shiny black shoes of public security, ladies' heels, baby sandals, flip-flops, and muddy bare feet. People stopped to peer in before continuing to the morning market.

She was troubled by the men's exchange in the office and by Xuan and the urn. She almost believed him that it held her father's ashes. She played on his respect for the dead and knew he would act his part. She sensed that he would not hurt her, but fat Pâté and Cross-eyed Lai were a different story. Was it possible that they were all in on it?

She waited. She told herself not to panic. JP and Na would come.

She remembered the note hours later when the sunlight faded into late afternoon and the surroundings were quiet. She retrieved the torn page from her pants pocket, unfolded it, and tried to make out JP's scribble in the dark.

Maia—Where are you? Na & I waited but we had to leave
early for the dock to take a ferry to the Swift Isle. Tonight, we'll
be at Love City Café. We were there last night while you were
sleeping. Guess who we ran into? Xuan and the Public Secu-
rity Trio, except they're no longer a trio—Comrade Ty is no
more. Pâté and Lai sang backup for Na, and the café's owner
wanted them back for a group audition. He liked the harmony
of their distinctive voices. I suggested they call themselves "Na
and the Hi-Los." The café was swarmed with American vets,
Taiwanese businessmen, and local government officials. Ev-
eryone wanted to feel Na's big hair and touch her smooth line-
less palms. If we don't catch up earlier, see you at Love City?
By the way, did you know that the Camel-less Troupe is also
in town? Apparently, we all caught the same Reunification
Express.—JP

Na and JP wouldn't miss her tonight. Maybe Xuan
would come. How did he know she was going to the Central Highlands? If he'd suspected, wouldn't he have stopped
her earlier? He'd asked her to return to Ho Chi Minh City.

Perhaps at a different time and place, they'd head south
on a daytime train, or ride it northbound on the brim of
the South China Sea, as JP said Theroux did in *The Great
Railway Bazaar*. They wouldn't stop at the capital but cross
the Red River into China at Lang Son. They'd ride to Bei-
jing, to Manchuria, where at Harbin, they'd go east into
the former U.S.S.R. They'd catch the *Trans-Siberian Express* at Ussurijsk, north to Chabarovsk, then westbound
for France. In France, Xuan would perfect his French and
meet a Parisian girl of Vietnamese descent. He'd use his
middle name, Vinh, for *honor* and *glory*, or he might just
keep Xuan—*spring* in Paris.

Around dinnertime, a young girl came with a bowl of rice and leafy green rau muống stir-fried in fermented bean curd. She did not step into the cell but placed the bowl and a pair of chopsticks on the ground. As she chained and padlocked the door, No-No slid in. He sniffed and wrinkled his nose at the stir-fried greens and then came up to Maia. He arched his back and rubbed against her legs a few seconds. He strutted toward the door and squeezed through underneath. That night he came back and curled up next to her, smelling both familiar and strange. He left before daybreak, leaving sandy paw prints on the bench.

On the second day, the girl brought her bag and a needle and yellow thread for the tear in Maia's shirt. Everything was still inside: wallet, Swiss Army knife, toiletry, first-aid kit, pen, and a pouch of dried leaves, berries, and barks.

"You'll be transferred tomorrow," the girl whispered and left quickly.

JP and Na did not come, nor did Xuan. That evening No-No did not slip in with the girl delivering dinner. Maia let the rice and silverfish sit untouched on the bench. It had been a day and a half and her stomach was churning, filling her mouth with a sour, bitter taste. She needed to clear her mind. She had not slept for thirty-six hours. Sleep. She needed sleep.

She reached for the pouch of dried herbs from the Isle Pagoda. Xuan and the Public Security Trio didn't know it was mixed in their tea, but she didn't get away, and they'd caught up with her. *A pinch for a restful night*, the old woman had instructed. *More than a pinch and you'll rest forever.* Comrade Ty got his dose, Maia thought to herself. *He no longer carries the burden.* Fatty and Cross-eyed got a good night's sleep, but Xuan was limping and twitchy.

She nibbled on a dry leaf that had a bitter aftertaste. She crumbled a pinch of leaves and berries like furikake over the rice and took a bite of the fried fishtail before swallowing a mouthful of rice. The salt and oil in the fish cut the bitterness. After the third bite, she began to feel better. Her stomach calmed, and the flavor of crispy fried silverfish filled her mouth. The dried leaves and berries tasted tangy and bittersweet like an unripe fruit.

She listened to the evening sounds of the nearby open market—no longer the morning buzz of early shoppers, the lull of afternoon nap, or the closing-up cacophony of bamboo brooms sweeping wet garbage into sewers, a stench that passed into the cell with the breeze. Nightfall came with the laughter of teenage boys, the roar of a motorcycle down an alley, the murmuring of lovers, the marching rhythm of a revolutionary song, sometimes a lullaby. As the human commotion came and went, leaving the rustle of leaves and chirping of crickets, she thought of her mother, of her letter from prison, of words she did not understand.

> *I am free, perhaps one of the happiest times of my life.*
> *I do not worry. My fate is in another's hands.*

Something did not feel right. She was weakened with nausea and spat out the half-eaten food that left her mouth salty and bitter. She was reminded of a quote she had copied in neat cursive in her high school journal—clear handwriting, round and resolute.

> *destiny is not a matter of chance*

it is a matter of choice
it is not a thing to be waited for
it is a thing to be achieved[14]

She could not sleep the night away. She could not wait for something to happen. Words from Old Seeker came to her: *Compose life, guess its riddles, and redeem its coincidences.* If she were to not fear the same life recurring but at its end shout, "from the beginning!" she must act.

Her eyes had become adjusted to the dull silvery light from the quarter moon that entered through the holes and cracks of the cell. Like the night, No-No slithered beneath the door and came to her. The cat sidled up for a belly rub, and her fingers began on his head, chin, and chest. Tonight, he smelled of Hawaiian Tropic and the briny sea, but there was something else, and then she remembered the evening air in the River of Nine Dragons when the travelers had a brew of sweet spices over the bonfire.

No-No purred, turning on his back, four paws in the air. She scratched his belly and he chortled. His navel seemed more swollen and warm. "Umbilical hernia," JP had said—his final diagnosis. "A protrusion of the stomach's stuff through the abdominal wall opening that would normally close, but it looks like the little fella has a delayed closure of the abdominal ring. Not a serious surgical operation. An American vet could repair it. Cut him open, push the bulge in, and sew him up. He'd go home the same day."

"The cat's going to America?" Na had asked JP.

"To the U.S. of A.," he had replied.

Umbilical hernia. Surgical operation. In the U.S. of A. And a plan came to Maia: *Cut him open. Push the bulge in.*

Sew him up. Cutting things did not faze her. She had dissected an earthworm in ninth grade, a frog in tenth, a guinea pig in eleventh, and a tomcat in her senior year. She wanted to be a coroner or an astronaut, an idea that came about after a space shuttle's explosion, a burst of flames across the sky. She was obsessed with death—her own and others'.

Her mind was already composing a letter to slip into No-No's belly.

She set her tools on the bench: hydrogen peroxide wipe, razor, Swiss Army knife, needle and thread, and bandage. She crumbled more leaves and berries onto the rice and placed the bowl under the cat's nose, clicking her tongue. "Come, boy," she cooed. "Come, boy—you'll sleep like a kitten." She forced a few crumbs through his clenched teeth. He hissed, bit her, and leapt from the bench. He settled in a far corner, licking himself and staring back.

The idea of being transferred in the morning began to sink in. She had heard stories of torture and recalled the warnings at a war crimes exhibition in Ho Chi Minh City.

> *Punish and Smash All Crimes and Criminals*
> *to Protect Vietnam's Independence,*
> *Social Order, Safety, and Territorial Integrity.*

She sat up, knocked the rice bowl onto the dirt, and staggered to the door, screaming into the silent night. "No! No! No!"

Dogs barked, someone cursed, but no one came.

She slumped on the ground.

Scurrying. Wrestling. Loud squeaks.

The cat leapt from the corner and pounced on something in the tipped rice bowl—a rat, a baby, its belly full of fish and rice. After a brief struggle, the rat went limp under No-No's paws; the victor gnawed at his captive.

The back of JP's note was blank. Torn from his journal, the five-by-eight-inch sheet could be folded in quarters, rolled tight like a joint, and wrapped in plastic. It'd be waterproof and almost indiscernible under the belly skin.

The silver moon through circles and slits provided enough light for her to make out the boundary of the paper's whiteness against the darkness. Soundless and stone-still, the cell began to feel tomblike. She steadied the pen between her quivering fingers and pressed its tip onto the blank page. She saw each word and space in her mind's eye—words imprinted from the briefings with the Coalition before her departure.

She had memorized the list of indictments: Communist Vietnam does not have peace and freedom but repression and fear. People's lives have not improved but worsened. They are living in poverty while Party members enjoy privileges they grant themselves for the years they sacrificed fighting. Vietnam is now run by men whose only experience is from fighting, not governing a country. Party members prosper; the masses live in destitution.

Each indictment could be authenticated by a personal tragedy. But the words left her with mixed emotions. There was something evolving at the edge, beyond her mission—a connectedness with others in the here and now. She grasped to pinpoint those feelings that made her less alone, that grounded her in relationships in a community.

She began her letter to JP Boyden.

The ballpoint rested on the space where she left off. Sitting upright on the bench, she slept and dreamed of the operation.

No-No, anesthetized and unconscious, sleeps with eyes half-open.

His belly's taut, the navel lump enormous. He seems to stare at her, but he's out, his back on the bench and four paws in the air. The double-bladed Gillette slides smoothly over wet tummy hair. She wipes the shaved rectangle with hydrogen peroxide. An inch above his navel, she punctures the skin lightly with the Swiss Army knife. Dark fluid oozes. He yowls loudly several times. She puts a finger over the cut to stop the flow. The liquid seeps under her finger and drenches the orange hair, dribbling over the bench onto the ground.

His eyes bother her. When her fingers move to close them, his eyelids shoot back up, and she drops the Swiss Army knife. Avoiding his stare, she retrieves the knife and makes a lengthwise two-inch incision over the navel. Warm liquid gushes over the bench and onto the ground, pooling around her ankles. She peels the skin back, separating it slightly from the stomach muscles. She's relieved. Just like chicken, she says to herself, but with chicken, there's not the pulsating liquid, not so much liquid beating with life.

Something moves beneath the abdominal wall. Umbilical hernia. A protrusion of the stomach's stuff, but JP didn't say it'd move as if it were alive. She makes a deeper incision where she's made the first and something bursts, oozing more dark fluid, and a feathered tail pokes out. She tugs at the tail. A sparrow slowly emerges, peeping softly. Soaking wet but invigorated by the release, the bird chirps louder, and from No-No's tummy, a flock of birds rises, beating their wings, slowly lifting from the throbbing slime that oozes from the belly over the bench and onto the floor, dark liquid surging to her knees, up to her chin.

She stands on the bench. The birds circle above. The cat floats to the surface, four legs spread eagle, and out of its stomach a woman backstrokes, the handles of a red basket looped around her shoulder. She treads in place in the pulsating ocean.

"Don't play with knives."

"It's an assignment, an operation."

"Your hair, do something." The woman gathers her own tresses that flow outward and knots them into a loose bun, all the while her legs pedaling as if on a bicycle. "I should visit a beauty salon myself," she says. "But today, off to the market for catfish soup." She floats on her back, then turns and dives through the opening beneath the door. Her hair unravels like seaweed.

"Liên Tỉnh Express Bus Station for ten đồng," a voice whispered. Padlock and chain rattled.

"Five," she replied. "Five đồng."

"Five đồng from Clouds Motel. It's farther from here. Ten đồng for two."

"Two?" She sat up and reached for No-No, but he was not there.

Scraping, a click, metal chain rattling, the door creaked open. Pale morning light passed into the cell. The xích lô boy stood at the door. "I borrowed the key from my sister."

Maia squinted past the boy at his xích lô. In the passenger seat sat a tall figure in dark peasant pants, a large woven basket in his lap. A straw cone hat hid his face.

"JP!" She rushed outside.

The neighborhood dogs, agitated by the sudden commotion, let out several yelps before falling back to sleep in the yards nearby. A rooster crowed in the distance as the ashen sky turned rosy on the eastern horizon. When the boy retrieved her bag and was about to lock the door, she stopped him and ran back inside to look for No-No.

"Hurry, Maia!" JP called. "He'll find his way."

"JP," she said, "you can't come with me."

The seaside town became visible under the gray morning light. The noises of early traffic and metal gates being rolled up filled the silence. The boy had already climbed onto his backseat, his hand resting on the thin rod that with a slight pull would release the brake.

"You'll stick out and draw attention."

"I'm heading for the Central Highlands," JP replied, "and you're returning to your birthplace, aren't you?" He grabbed her hand, and with a strong pull, she was next to him. "Besides, you'll be safer with me."

The Cliff

THE XÍCH LÔ boy pulled up beside a tree stump and hopped off his seat. He lifted the rear to lower the front for JP and Maia to step off. "They won't find you here," the boy said.

Their hideout was a small earthen shack that clung to a boulder on a cliff overlooking the South China Sea. The shack had a rusty tin roof and three makeshift walls. The fourth was the boulder that the shack clung to. The boulder sloped into a plateau of smaller stones, where tough grass grew in crevices, and then plunged steeply into the sea. Here, on the northern outskirts of Nha Trang, the boy lived with his young sister.

The late morning sun rose, but the cliff was breezy and cool, with a sticky sea mist in the air. "That's the Isle of the Swifts." JP pointed to a hilly island in the distance. "We were there, Na and me."

Maia lay on the pebbly ground, arching her back over a smooth protruding stone. "What now?" she asked herself.

JP stretched his back over the large rock beside her and lifted his feet straight up. The cramped hour-long xích lô escape from the bus station had left their bodies aching, with kinks in their sore muscles. None of the buses would take foreigners. When they tried to bribe a driver with U.S. dollars, he threatened to report them to public security.

The boy returned from the shack with a plate of assorted fruits that included a soursop, kumquats, wi apples, guavas, and starfruit and a dish of salt and chili. He had to pedal xích lô for the day, but they could stay until they found a way out of Nha Trang.

"Riding South with Northern Mothers" was a caption JP had been mulling over since the morning he saw the women and the yellow Russian bus. Checking into Clouds Motel, the group would not meet his eyes when he approached them. Their old eyes glazed over when Na translated his wish. They did not want an American to accompany them on their southward journey to past battlegrounds where they hoped to excavate and bring home the remains of their sons and daughters.

"I could see anger in their eyes," JP told Maia.

They had eaten the fruits and climbed down to the shore, sitting on a mossy boulder, their feet touching the crashing waves. JP was silent for a long time. "See this?" He pulled up his shirtsleeve to reveal the faded tattoo. "My half-brother was deployed to 'Nam in '66." His voice cracked, but she kept silent. "We've lost, too," he said. "MIA, last seen in Pleiku. Sometimes I think he defected, AWOL, living somewhere. He questioned the war. He was angry when his buddies took me to Waikīkī to get this before their deployment." JP touched the insignia on his arm. "This lightning bolt."

The xích lô boy did not return until late afternoon the next day. His young sister was perched in the passenger seat with groceries, enough for a party of eight. Two shiny red Honda Dream motorcycles trailed the xích lô. Na was driving Xuan on one, and the public security duo was on the other.

"Girl!" Na called. "Xuan has something for you."

Her father's ashes, Maia thought as she and JP watched from the shack where they had spent the night, still trying to figure a way out of Nha Trang. Her heart did not quicken when she realized they had company. Pâté and Lai were almost unrecognizable out of their public security uniforms. Though weak from hunger, dizzy from the heat, and feeling heavy from listening to JP, she was neither apprehensive nor alarmed. She felt an inexplicable lightness in seeing the group. JP also seemed relieved that their conversation had been interrupted.

"A feast," Na announced. "Pan-fried trout in ginger fish sauce, lotus-stalk salad with steamed prawns and sliced pig ears, summer squash soup, and parboiled taro leaves dipped in chili anchovy sauce."

The boy ran off to sweep the plank veranda. His sister, smiling shyly at Maia, showed them to the open-air kitchen. The girls were in charge of preparing dinner. "A farewell party!" Na said, high-spirited with her latest singing gig and Xuan's news. Her skills at extracting information from individuals and then piecing together the details were ingenious, her delight in the moment infectious.

By early evening, they sat cross-legged around the meal spread out on the plank veranda. "Let's toast," the xích lô boy said. "To new friends and good food."

Na laughed. "To old friends and a new beginning." She clinked cups with Pâté and Lai, who had resigned from public security. The new trio had accepted advance payments to headline as *Na and the Hi-Los* at Love City Café.

"We're traveling to compete in the upcoming Highlands' talent show!" Pâté announced.

"To the past," Xuan said. "Let it be."

JP raised his cup. "To future adventures."

The dinner's conversation began with why the shack was erected where it was—suspended in midair, hanging off a cliff, its veranda creaking in the wind.

"The Isle of the Swifts," the boy's sister said softly. "Our father liked to watch the swiftlets swerving in twilight."

"The locals harvested bird nests on that island," the boy said. "A kilo fetches hundreds of dollars in the black market, but it's too dangerous to climb down the rocks."

"Swifts, sea swallows, salanganes—same thing?" JP asked.

"Harvesting bird nests is not more dangerous than fishing," Na said. "I heard that the orange, pink, and red—the rarer kinds—fetch more. Then you can leave this place." She laughed. "Though I love the sway." She flung her hands about as if waving a conductor's baton, directing the ensemble of shack and wind.

"You can learn how to scale those rocks," JP said, bright-eyed from the blood-warm rice wine. "Once you get the technique, it's pretty methodical, but you need proper equipment."

"How do you know? You know how?" Na gulped the last of her wine and turned to Maia. "Xuan has something for you."

Xuan dug into his pocket, took out a stone ring, and held it out to Maia. "It's Na's idea."

"The stone of springtime," Na said, "from the Marble Mountains."

"Na and the Hi-Los had it set on the ring for you," Xuan said. "Paid for from their first advance."

"Little Sister," Pâté said, "it's a reminder that we'll always be with you."

"You're not alone," Lai said.

Na slipped the ring onto Maia's finger. "It's a perfect fit!" The flat, almost circular stone was rough, with lines, pock- marks and crevices, like a moon.

"Very nice." JP studied the stone. "White marble from the Marble Mountains? Gravestones and souvenirs."

"What?" Na said.

"The marble shops sell gravestones to the locals and sou- venirs to the tourists."

Na slapped him.

Without looking at Xuan, Maia knew the stone was from the girl he met by the riverbank on the trail.

"Xuan is leaving with the Camel-less Troupe," Na an- nounced. "They're smuggling him out in their box, and No- No is going, too."

After the feast, the xích lô boy led the group in gathering dried branches and bark to twist into a two-ply rope to prac- tice rappelling off the rocky cliff. Xuan and Maia stood un- der the quarter moon overlooking the sea. They could hear JP and Na and the Hi-Los hooting with excitement.

"Na has the ashes," Xuan said, "until you decide."

"What if those are not my father's?" she blurted out. "What if there was a mistake at the crematory in South Philly? Na sees a black man."

"Come with me, Mai."

He whispered so quietly she had to turn to him. "With Old Seeker and the motley others? Why?"

"You're free! You don't need to do anything. This regime will disintegrate."

"Is that why you're leaving?"

"My family left after the war. I stayed because we fought for so long. I waited. I understand now that I must leave in order to return. Besides—" He gazed at her. "If I stay longer, I might fall in love."

"Where will you go?"

He laughed. "Not many obeyed the three delays during the war, we didn't." His eyes were distant. "Why are you?"

"What happened to the girl—?"

He shook his head before she could finish the question. "Do you know why your parents named you Hoàng Mai?"

"It's a Vietnamese Mickey Mouse flower."

"Is that what you want to believe?" He was about to say something but then changed his mind. After a pause, he said, "I'm thinking China, the Soviet Union, France, or America."

She looked up at the night sky.

"It'll always be with you," he said. "The faithful moon."

Early the next morning after everyone left, JP proposed a plan to Maia.

"We'll leave Nha Trang on bicycles. We'll bike to Ninh Hoa on Highway 1."

She nodded sleepily, feeling lightheaded from the night before. She turned the stone ring around and around on her finger.

"Because of the killer hills," he continued, "we'll hitch-hike Route 26 toward the mountains, crossing rivers and passing villages with names like . . . like . . ."

"M'Đrăk, Ea Krông Búk, and Krông Pắk." She played along. "We'll reverse the retreat of 1975!"

"What?"

"Nothing."

"Let's stay here for another day," he said. "We'll take off at daybreak on our one-speed made-in-China bicycles. We ride north toward a fat rubicund sun that rises over the horizon between blue and blue."

"You know, JP Boyden, I've heard that before."

"Right. 'Where one may float between blue and blue,' George Eliot's *Daniel Deronda*." He scribbled in his embossed leather travelogue. "But this is *our* story." He flipped backward to the first page. "As with all stories, it begins with a chance meeting." He smiled at her. "Or is it fate?"

The Shuttle

AT DAYBREAK, THEY left Nha Trang on bicycles and pedaled north on National Highway 1 along the coast. As the sun rose and fog dissipated, the Truong Son Range became visible in the west. When the wind blew from the east, they would smelled the briny South China Sea.

"This way," JP called out to Maia, "we can see the country."

The traffic drew around them like a traveling circus act. A man on a Vespa decelerated to practice his English. A woman in a xích lô with a basketful of groceries invited them to her home for breakfast. A boy on a bicycle too big for him stood on his pedals, pushing hard to match their speed. "Hello, Liên Xô! Hello, Liên Xô!" He grinned at JP, his white shirttail flapping in the sultry wind.

They rode with the rise and fall of the winding highway. They stopped for warm baguettes and fromage and iced café au lait. They made detours onto dirt paths to see how people lived. They ate fish and rice for lunch at a family cơm bình dân and swam in the sea. They rested a while under coconut palms as the sun grew unbearably hot. Then they were off again. When they became disoriented from the heat and queasy from eating unfamiliar street food, they crashed by the roadside and vomited. They continued north.

They made thirty-something kilometers after an all-day ride and reached the T-junction of the highway and Route 26. Exhausted, aching, and sunburnt, they got off their bicycles and stood under the dusky sky. They scanned the deserted juncture as night arrived and realized they had miscalculated the time and distance.

"We go west from here." Maia pointed to the shadowy upslope to the highlands.

A few hundred yards beyond the juncture, a faint yellow light flickered in the wind. They pushed their bicycles toward the illumination and found a spacious tin roof structure, its entrance without a door and its windows without curtains. Rusty metal tables and chairs filled the airy eatery yet there was not a single customer. A teenage girl was placing round aluminum trays of food on the tables. Each tray consisted of the same dishes: rice, dark stewed meat and hardboiled eggs, lettuce and herbs, pickled vegetables, and chili fish sauce.

JP's greeting "Chao em!" startled the girl, who grinned when she saw him and called him "Uncle!" before vanishing from the dining room. She returned with her mother carrying a glowing oil lantern.

The woman raised the lantern near JP's face. "He does look like your Ba's friend."

"Are you serving dinner?" Maia asked.

"The food looks stale," JP whispered in Maia's ear.

"We can make something else for you," the woman said.

The girl took JP's hand and led them to the well in the back to wash up. They passed the family's bare living quarters—a đi văng by a curtainless window and a modest dresser on which a black-and-white framed photograph sat.

"Má said that's my Ba." The girl bowed her head to the youth in a crisp ARVN uniform in the picture.

When they returned, the girl told them that their meal would be ready in a moment and seated them at a table near the kitchen, where they could hear the sizzling of cooking.

The girl flitted from table to table to light joss sticks. Soon the place was hazy with incense smoke.

The woman brought out a tray of food for Maia and JP—rice, dark stewed meat and hardboiled eggs, lettuce and herbs, pickled vegetables, and chili fish sauce. "Please, eat."

Maia avoided JP's eyes.

The woman pulled a chair up to their table, sat down, and started a conversation. She watched as JP tried to poke the leathery egg with his chopsticks. She told them what they already knew: foreigners were not allowed on the Central Highlands.

"We'll bike there," JP said, "in the moonlight."

"He's kidding, isn't he?" she asked Maia. The woman sliced the egg into quarters for JP.

"Is there a place to spend the night around here?" Maia asked.

"If you'd like, you can rest on the đi văng," the woman said. "There's a shuttle to the highlands that comes at midnight. I'll send the girl to alert you when it arrives."

Jasmine incense filled the family's living quarters, making the air thick and heavy. JP took off his *L'amant* T-shirt and batted at the mosquitoes, generating air like a low-speed fan. Their tired bodies welcomed the smooth wooden surface of the plank-bed.

Pale moonlight passed through the naked window.

"There's a lake atop a mountain where the earth and sky meet, where you can touch that cool silver moon," Maia said.

"Where would that be?"

"In my father's letter to my mother."

"Is that a real place?"

"My father could've made it up. He regretted that he and my mother didn't meet by the lake for a date."

"You don't want to regret not having time together."

"Did you pluck the moment?"

"Na is a lot of fun. She's all there." He stopped fanning. "But you, I don't understand. You're—"

"Inscrutable?"

"I wouldn't say that." He studied her silently. "You speak English."

"Oh, thank you."

"Sometimes I think I understand you, but then I don't. It's as if you're all cut up under that composure." He started fanning again. "What's with you and Xuan? Why was he following you?"

"He's not following me anymore, is he?"

"He likes you."

"He's not available. He's *delayed*—"

"That's interesting. He said that about you."

"I am not."

"You're not available."

"Why? Are you interested?"

He leaned close to her. "Do you know that portentous things happen when the moon is not quite full?"

They fell into a silence as if waiting, listening.

Then they heard a distant rumbling.

"Like that?" she asked.

They listened to something massive coming down from the highlands. The unexpected din at midnight sent chills up their spines.

JP put on his shirt. "That's a six-cylinder diesel engine."

The air in the room, just cleared of jasmine incense, was now filled with an overwhelming stench of decay and blood as the rumbling increased, gradually deafening and then screeching to a stop. They heard an army of feet and voices entering the diner. The girl came to tell them that the shuttle had arrived.

Their ride was the remnants of a badly burned truck. The driver was the youth in the picture from the dresser. When he approached, Maia noticed his uniform was bloodstained. The smell of blood, diesel, and smoke made her nauseous, and she held onto JP, who stood awestruck in front of the battered 10-tire vehicle with a covered cargo bed. Patches of camouflage paint remained where the truck was not scorched.

"We should ride our bikes," she said.

The driver and JP shook hands like two old friends.

"We'll collect a few passengers along the way," the youth said. "You'll be on the Central Highlands in no time."

"Come, Maia." JP headed for the crew cab. "You can take the window seat."

The youth was already at the steering wheel. JP climbed into the cabin and pulled her up beside him. He whispered, "She's an M35 Deuce and a Half!"

They left Ninh Hoa, heading for the highlands on Route 26.

The blaring music was cranked up high, and the wind whipped through the truck, yet the smell lingered. She hung her head out of the window to breathe.

She heard voices. What with the tape player and the howling wind, she first thought they were coming from outside. The driver and JP were talking in a low conversational tone. When she listened more closely, the voices sounded as if they were singing along with the taped music—sometimes harmonizing, other times off-key, sometimes in a group, other times a resounding solo.

She finally asked the driver, "Who's singing?"

He cranked up the tape player. "Nhạc này cô nghe được không?"

She turned the music down and heard the singing continue from the cargo bed.

"Are there people in the back?"

The driver was silent for a moment. Then he said, "Some boarded and haven't gotten off, riding back and forth, no destination."

The truck suddenly screeched to a halt. The driver got out, and JP followed him through the driver's door. Moments later she heard the rear gate slam and then a disturbance on the truck bed. JP and the driver returned, and they continued.

They stopped several more times. Each time the smell of smoke, blood, and rotten flesh became more unbearable, making it hard to breathe in the cab. Her nausea worsened.

Near daybreak, they picked up a young highlander, who squeezed in the cab with them. Wearing blood-soaked fatigues, he brought with him an overwhelming stench from a festering open wound, but JP did not seem to mind. They exchanged stories—JP from books and the soldier from experience. They eagerly filled each other's gaps; piece-by-piece, a picture emerged.

"How much farther to Phoenix Pass?" Maia asked the driver, raising her voice over JP and the soldier's exchange.

"After the next bend."

"Please let me off at Phoenix Pass."

JP and the soldier stopped talking. "Why Phoenix Pass?" JP asked, turning to her, noticing her paleness and sweat.

"Are you feeling okay? You look like you're about to throw up."

"From Phoenix Pass, I can get to the Vong Phu Mountain."

"That is the shortcut," the Montagnard soldier confirmed.

The driver met JP's eyes in the rearview mirror. "You'll stay on until Pleiku, won't you? It's still quite a way. Plus, we can use your advice."

"Tell me again, what's at the Vong Phu Mountain?" JP looked hard at Maia.

"I'm collecting oral stories on Hòn Vọng Phu. And no, you cannot come along, and no, I am not accompanying you as your translator to Pleiku."

The truck turned sharply on a switchback and skidded to a stop.

"Mai'a," JP whispered, "sweet banana." He wrapped his arms around her. "I'll see you again by the lake atop a mountain where earth meets sky."

Not looking at him, she climbed off the shuttle, which pulled away without delay and disappeared around the winding path.

She threw up until she was empty.

Five

Phoenix Pass

A WAXING GIBBOUS moon hung palely at daybreak.

"Whatever you do," the Independent Vietnam Coalition had instructed, "be at the foot of the Vong Phu Mountain on the first night of the full moon."

Suspended between verdant valleys and cloudy peaks, Maia walked on Phoenix Pass. She wanted to measure each step and feel the ground beneath her feet, but when the nausea worsened and she felt lightheaded, she hailed a passing motorcyclist.

"Going to the mountain, miss?" A weathered taxi-motorbiker slowed down beside her. "Which one?"

She pointed to a misty peak on the Western Range.

She knew the peak's many names. In a travel atlas published in-country, the mountain on which Hòn Vọng Phu stood was labeled by its popular Sino-Vietnamese name, "Núi Vọng Phu," Waiting for Husband Mountain. A folklore collection referred to it as "Núi Mẫu Tử," Sino-Vietnamese for Mother and Child Mountain; in French, "La Mère et l'Enfant." In an old edition, the mountain bore its indigenous name, "Chư Mư," or Wife Mountain in Jarai. She had heard the local folks call it "Núi Mẹ Bồng Con."

"Could you take me to the Mother Cradling Child Mountain?"

"I can get you to the nearest town," the man said, "though you might not see the original stone peak. The local quarries are operating day and night to supply rock for home and road construction."

She shook her head and refused a ride, not believing his story.

"Well, stay out of the sun," he warned, "or you'll burn charred black like a block of wood." Engine revving loudly, he disappeared around the winding pass.

She continued on foot. The man could have told the truth, she thought, recalling a California reporter's claim that Hòn Vọng Phu had shattered and crumbled into the South China Sea.[15] She questioned that news report, too.

When the sun blazed at noon and moisture evaporated, she reeled off the burning paved path and found a grove of young trees, whose exposed roots entwined into a cradle-like nook. She sat down, shielded from the heat and enclosed in silence.

She had returned only in time for her grandmother's wake. She accepted that her mother was lost at sea. The past unfurled and then coiled into a tight ball. Learning the details of her mother's life made the woman she called Má real. But she could no longer remember the time when she spoke the word *Má* aloud.

She thought about her yearning for a home, and doubt began to seep through her. What was the possibility of making contact with her great-aunt, a woman whom she had never met, a woman who assumed the alias "Black Fairy"? If she were to believe what she had read or just heard, Hòn Vọng Phu might have fragmented and become a foundation for a home or been dispersed across the sea. If this were a dream, would she pinch herself awake?

She should have listened to her friend Phat in Little Saigon telling her the story of a man who was dreaming he was a butterfly.

Or was it a butterfly dreaming it was a man?

"Am I in a dream?" she whispered to the stillness of midday. And whose dream—my own or another's?

Somewhere, a melody played, like the offbeat chorus from the midnight shuttle. The tune echoed, as if coming from beneath the earth or above treetops. A cacophony of voices surrounded her, a lively harmony, first faint and then loud and clear.

She thought of Na and the Hi-Los just before their sparkly red Honda Dreams zoomed by, Na on one and the Hi-Los on the other. She remembered they were traveling to the highlands' songfest. Na's windblown hair, the Hi-Los' blue jeans and T-shirts, and their singing in the wind had a gusto that Maia wished she could let go and be a part of.

As the sound of their engines became muffled by distance, she heard the sputter of another vehicle. The trike motorcycle-cartman slowly passed by, towing a finished boat with what first appeared like a cabin but in reality was the waterlogged wooden crate falling apart, wide cracks revealing a shadow within. Xuan gazed out through the slats.

She was reminded of the lines her father once recited from a self-help guide found at a used bookstore: *Two men looked out from prison bars. One saw the mud . . . the other saw stars.*[16] A deep ache for her Ba overcame her. She understood he saw his life as a prison and tried to seek freedom from within. What imprisoned him? What freed him? If life were his prison cell, what were his stars?

On the path, she saw Old Seeker with No-No at his side, tawny and lionlike, and the motley others parading by. The fruit boy twirled the stolen rearview mirror, a sudden blinding flash of illumination. Perhaps she could join their restless search for answers—to ask questions, to learn from their lived experiences. Perhaps they could make sense of her purpose, help her find a way to string together a life of chances and choices, to see a beginning and an end. The soporific heat weighed on her like a blanket as she watched the parade head west. She closed her eyes to the glaring noon light. When she woke, it was in the grayness of the next morning.

Maia continued across the barren land. She walked westward on Phoenix Pass until she came to a T-junction. She turned north onto a provincial road leading to a small town on the western flank of the range. She passed farmers tilling the earth that produced nothing but backbreaking labor. Fording a side stream, she arrived at the foot of the mountain. She stopped in front of the last thatched hut. A sliver of the full moon peeped from behind evening rainclouds.

A thin white-haired man emerged from the hut.

"Is that the Vong Phu Mountain?" she asked.

The man was silent.

She recited the lines she had memorized:

> *A crane flies—*
> *cloudy peak, still water*
> *a shadow awaits.*

He searched her face, as if looking for someone. "Where did you hear that?" His accent told her he was a native of the coastal plains of central Vietnam.

"From overseas friends of the poet."

"I composed those lines during the war."

"For my Great-Aunt E. Tien."

His expression softened. "Black Fairy," he murmured. Raindrops splashed on the dirt road. "I will take you to the Moon Fest."

Moon Fest

MIDSUMMER NIGHTS WHEN the moon was full, people would gather atop the Vong Phu Mountain to celebrate the Moon Fest. The poet insisted on taking his single-speed bicycle even though it was pouring rain. "Not to worry," he assured Maia, his small figure shrouded in an oversized gray poncho. He straddled the bicycle and gestured her to climb on the backseat and get under his cloak. "We'll get as close as possible to the trailhead and hike the rest of the way."

Inside the poncho, as if blindfolded and hidden from view, Maia held onto the poet as he maneuvered the slippery circuitous pass—now this way, now that way, around and around. Eventually, he could not pedal further. He grunted. When the bicycle threatened to slide backward, they got off and pushed it uphill until they reached a trail of unattended vehicles: old vans, trucks, farm tractors, makeshift trailers. The poet left his bicycle beside a wooden vessel attached to a motorcycle.

He gripped her hand and pulled her up the mountain. All around, people were making the climb. They could not see faces but heard code-switching and mixing between various tongues of the lowlands and highlands. Here and there, red embers of cigarettes dotted the meandering trail. After many twists and turns on the muddy slope of intertwined dead roots, then stones, and finally boulders, they could see blazing bonfires and moving lanterns illuminating the misty peak. They heard music.

The Moon Fest was in full swing when they arrived. A large canopy shielded the center stage from the pouring rain. Surrounded by bonfires and people carrying colorful paper lanterns, the stage lit the night.

"Welcome to *Highlands Got Talent*!" the stout emcee greeted the audience. At his side was a gesticulating simian.

Maia looked at the poet in disbelief.

"The Black Fairy attends every year," he said.

"Three nights of competition," the emcee explained. "As always, the themes are departing, waiting, and returning. Tonight, it's departing. Our first contestants hail from the marble stone village."

A group of eight children in crimson garb performed an intricate lantern dance, followed by a band of husband, wife, and child, playing a lively piece on the monochord zither, long zither, and bamboo flute. An aging crooner from the Mekong delivered a grief-stricken vọng cổ rendition of Hòn Vọng Phu.

"I think my friends are here," Maia whispered.

The poet led her from the canopy into the rain. Away from the light, she noticed tents of different sizes and shapes on the peak's shadowy fringe. They visited the tents to inquire about the Black Fairy. People spoke in various Montagnard tongues that Maia did not understand. Their impassioned voices reminded her of the night at the motorcycle-cartman's home.

A sudden pounding of gongs and drumbeats reverberated through the rain. The familiar marching rhythm drew Maia's attention back to the center stage, on which a trio in traditional highland wear was performing. The woman in the middle was clapping a cymbal, flanked by a chubby rice drummer and a thin man beating a large gong with a mallet.

They banged the indigenous instruments in the rhythm of a French military band that at times echoed the Russian Red Army marching song, "Katyusha."

"Those are my friends!" Maia said and rushed toward the stage to see Na and the Hi-Los up close. The trio sang in unison the first "Hòn Vọng Phu" by Lê Thương.

> the king orders the army depart, drums beating
> along the river over the mountain, flags fly
> farewell drinks, happy songs: a husband goes ten thousand miles
> a wife awaits in shadow of wind and dust[17]

The drumbeat and gongs stirred the audience. Hundreds of feet marched in place and the ground trembled. Maia stepped in time with the people around her, feeling the inevitable tragedy of war. Beside her, the poet stood stone still.

"Your great-aunt departed with the army," he said and led Maia from the crowd. They left the canopy and walked into the rain.

"We were classmates at the Collège de Qui Nhon. I was a student of classical literature, she was history. We had many long discussions about our futures. We were young and idealistic. We both wanted the same for our country. I remained in the South, and she joined the Viet Minh. Like many highlanders, she fought for the Liberation of the Central Highlands, a promise yet to be realized.

"It's said that lowlanders and highlanders are brothers and sisters, that we can live together on our ancestral land, free in the mountain, but that's not so. In the end, we're tilling the same lot of barren earth."

Na and the Hi-Los concluded the first round of competition. People dispersed from the light into the pouring
darkness. There was no sign of her great-aunt.

"Perhaps the rain has delayed her," the poet said.

On the second night, the heavy downpour doused several
small bonfires. Under a veiled moonlight and shrouded in
a floating mist, the peak turned dark and vaporous. People
abandoned their dripping wet paper lanterns but still huddled around the center stage.

The competition opened with a boy blowing a leaf horn,
the quiet soulful notes barely audible above the rain. The
poet, sinking into melancholy, confided in Maia. "We
fought and made sacrifices, but here we are still waiting for
the promised peace and harmony."

On stage, a woman plucked a two-string moon lute and
crooned "Hòn Vọng Phu 2."

> why wait?
> reunion will come
> rain seeps into the soul
> mountains gather and form the western range
> trees, flowers, and streams urge: do not let spring pass
> islands keep watch for the return
> nine great dragons carry words
> a thousand years pass before reaching the waiting stone[18]

"Your great-aunt didn't wait," the poet said. "She went
north and fought for the revolution. She fell in love with
its leader."

"Uncle Ho?"

Something flickered in the poet's eyes. "When a child was born, the boy was sent to her village to be cared for by others."

"My second cousin?"

"Dead. Burned alive in the crossfire of war." The poet steadied the rising tension in his voice. "She kept fighting. Only afterward did she realize the promise of independence was a lie. We were chess pieces moved by more powerful players. We believed we were fighting for our own ideals, but were we?" He looked at her. "What were we fighting for? What are you fighting for? Tell me!"

She did not have a thought-out answer. She marched to the drumbeat of South Vietnamese expatriates to carry out what she envisioned was her father's wish. She supported the Coalition unquestioningly and bore its slogan: *Down with Communism! Democracy for Vietnam!* She knew stories of those who fought and died for their beliefs.

But did she have the zeal to kill or die?

She thought of her father and his fight. Perhaps, like her father, she was not made of the kind of heroism that war called for. She wished to live as equally as she wished for others to live. She realized what moved her was living for what she loved.

She asked, "What is the shape of one's life when one's action is based on love?"

The poet gazed at her, his eyes distant. "Your great-aunt will be here tomorrow. It's the finale of returning."

The rain let up on the third night. The full moon came out, illuminating the barren peak in a silvery light. The makeshift shelters on the outskirts dissipated with the fog. Maia learned that they were not standing on the Vong Phu

Mountain. From where they were, they could discern the silhouette of the mother cradling her child on the next peak.

"No one has reached them," the poet said. "They can only be seen from a distance."

Maia also learned that her great-aunt did not attend the festival that year.

"It's not like her to miss the event," the poet repeated as they questioned others on her whereabouts.

On stage, under the starry sky, renditions of returning were playing out. An odd pair of performers pierced the night with animal-like calls. One sported ripped Levi's and Ranchero Stars and Stripes boots, pale as a ghost; the other was charred black, barely covered with a loincloth and shaking a brightly painted bamboo tube. The shrill cries of the black-shanked douc, songs of the golden-winged laughingthrush, and hiss of the water monitor filled the audience with a deep yearning for reconnection. People retreated within themselves and listened to the beating of their own hearts atop the bare peak, momentarily transformed into a lush forest. As the last note echoed, the audience slowly emerged from the feast of silence.

The odd pair bowed and vanished into the night. The next act took the stage, but people no longer paid attention. They milled about restlessly, debating the current situation of the Central Highlands. They could not be pushed further from their ancestral land. They must act, or they would turn into stone, waiting. Many had fought for the North, trusting that the highlands would be liberated and the indigenous would be free to live in the mountains after the fight. Instead, they were pawned and now forced to relocate further into the uncultivable jungle. They must rise up in order to return home.

The momentum of time made it urgent to find her great-aunt. Amid the frenzy, Maia saw a deep inner conflict, one that she needed to rethink and reconcile. To her surprise, the person she thought who might understand her was JP Boyden. She had not truly listened when he told her about his brother. She realized that she and JP were both searching for what was lost. Were they wishing for the impossible—to go back to a time before the war? Were they seeking the past to extend it into the present? Did they have other choices?

She wanted to tell JP that his losing a brother and his hope that he might still be alive somewhere linked their lives. She wanted to tell him that his brother's refusal to fight was a recognition of others, of kinship.

The last performers were drowned out by the heated deliberations of the audience. The songs and dances on stage became white noise for feverish talk of an organized demonstration to voice the people's discontent.

In the midst of the chatter and jubilation about a clear resolution, the poet managed to obtain information on the Black Fairy's whereabouts. He passed the directions on to Maia and bade her to go quickly before the mass descent from Waiting Mountain. He disappeared into the crowd that pulsated like the beating heart of a caged animal ready to spring.

Legitimacy

LEE HAKAKU BOYDEN anticipated the sea change long before Vinnie and Kai returned from the Moon Fest with news of unrest on the Central Highlands.

"Tension is rising between the highlanders and Hanoi," Vinnie reported. "The people are planning a demonstration. We must act."

"What should we do?" Kai asked.

"We do nothing," Lee replied. "We observe the boundaries as we've been doing."

"We infiltrate from the western border," Vinnie proclaimed. "We overthrow the Communists and bring democracy to the people. Hanoi is preoccupied with the crisis on the highlands. Now is the time to strike. We can't wait for directives from overseas."

"It's one jungle," Kai said. "Where are the borders?"

Quietly, Kai considered the options: to remain uninvolved, inhabiting the in-between, or to stand up and fight for the oppressed. Was it a simple question of to fight or not to fight? Was there a third path?

He felt warmth stirring within, ignited the day they came upon the children by the lake. Vinnie teased him that it was love, that his true love's kiss would break the curse of hellfire and wake Sleeping Beauty, and they'd all live happily ever after.

The strong pull Kai felt toward the children made him question his origin. He was named Kai for Lee's yearning for the sea that surrounded his home in the Pacific, but he was found in the fire. His name was a contradiction. His beginning was lost.

How could such a life be legitimate?

"Who am I?" he asked. "What am I to do?"

Homecoming

MAIA REACHED THE outskirts of the Central Highlands in late morning. The poet's directions for locating her great-aunt were straightforward. From Waiting Mountain, go northwest toward the border of Vietnam and Cambodia. Beyond the outermost town's open market, wooden church, and footbridge, cut through the thorny honey locust forest to a clear stretch of barren land. On a plateau behind a bamboo fence, look for a thatched longhouse with square windows.

"You'll know when you've arrived."

The dwelling sat on red dirt amid overgrown tussocks and bamboo. The place was quiet except for the wind ruffling tall grass, a stream flowing over rocks nearby, and an occasional whistling that sounded like a child or wild dog.

She walked along the bamboo fence to a latched gate and let herself in. She crossed the bare dirt yard and followed the smell of cooking to an open area behind the house. An elderly woman on her haunches with her back toward Maia was fanning several fires. Over the fires were a pot of rice and barley, a pot of dark green leafy vegetable soup, and a pot of stewed meat.

"The bowls, please," the woman said without looking around.

Maia hesitated. The woman stood up and turned. It was her great-aunt. Her head was shaved, but Maia recognized her strong features. She had lost the softness of youth and was gaunt in old age, accentuating her intense eyes.

"You're not my helper from town."

"I can help."

Her great-aunt directed her to line up the large plastic soup bowls on the ground. "You're family, aren't you?"

"I am your great-niece."

"You must be my older sister's—"

"Granddaughter."

"How is your grandmother?"

"She passed away."

"Was she unwell?"

"It was her time."

"You don't want to go too early or too late."

"She planted the fruit of her desire, but I don't know what that is."

"She did her part. But me—?" Her great-aunt stoked the fire, making embers glow and ashes fly.

"I have words from the Independent Vietnam Coalition."

Her great-aunt did not seem to hear. Instead, she fluffed the rice and barley, stirred the soup and meat, and began to assemble the meal. In each bowl, she put a scoop of rice and barley, poured a ladle of vegetable soup, and sprinkled bits of salty meat on top.

As soon as the last bowl was prepared, Maia heard twittering and saw movement in the bamboo thicket. A group of mud-covered children came through, carrying a variety of makeshift farm tools. They stopped at the stone well to wash up before gathering around the outdoor kitchen.

The children were mostly teenagers. From a distance, they appeared normal, but a closer look revealed that each had something odd. An elfin girl with long hair came for the bowls and helped to serve others. Her lack of eyes made her seem as if she were sleepwalking. A brown lanky boy pranced along with a twisted torso, walking on all fours. A child without arms nimbly clutched the bowl with the arches of her feet. The boy without legs propped himself against another child to balance upright. One had a head much bigger than the bowl, another far smaller, both with ogling fishlike eyes. The teenager with the shakes cradled a blood red bundle.

Great-Aunt told the teenager to give it to Maia.

"I'm Binh." The teenager introduced himself and held out the bundle. "This is the fifth meat born to the lieutenant's family. It's called Sixth Kabāb." Binh grinned broadly. "Don't make Sixth Kabāb cry."

When the little one was placed in Maia's arms, it woke, panicked, and wetted her. Binh gestured Maia to rock it back and forth. She was given its bowl. The children sat on the ground, eating and conversing like a flock of birds. The nursling was calm after the initial panic. Its mouth opened and chewed slowly every spoonful of food, not making a peep.

After the meal, the children worked on their assigned tasks in the silence of midday. Some practiced their penmanship while others read to themselves.

"Do you have a lesson for the children?" Great-Aunt asked Maia.

"A lesson?"

"Neither the kitchen help nor the children's teacher came today. Something must have kept them. Did you notice anything unusual in town on your way here?"

"No."

"They're volunteers from public security, coming and going on a regular basis, keeping watch over this orphanage."

Great-Aunt was sitting beside the child without arms, helping her with the spacing between the characters. With the pencil wedged between her warped toes, the child continued to inscribe over a single space, character upon character.

As Maia watched her overlay one character on top of another, she recalled the dwarf's inscription. She wanted to ask whether it was Chinese, Sino-Vietnamese, Cyrillic, or a combination of all those scripts, and what it meant.

"Well?" Great-Aunt peered at her.

"I don't have a lesson."

"Everyone has a lesson. The children can't travel. Whenever a traveler passes through, we ask for a lesson. They might be bound to their small lot, but they're a part of a larger world. Learning from travelers will help them become aware of others and understand that an individual's action affects the whole. What knowledge have you carried from afar?"

Seeing the children losing themselves in the tasks at hand, Maia hesitated. Their concentration enveloped the moment in serenity. She held back the message from overseas. She would speak with Great-Aunt when they were alone.

"I have stories and songs for the children."

"Then you can tell a story and teach them a song."

The children gathered around Maia, and Kabāb was placed again in her arms. Rocking the bundle to and fro, she told stories she had accumulated—stories from her father, stories she read in school, stories of rocks. Talking animals made the children happy, so she told an animal fantasy and taught them a bit of song.

That night Maia slept in the hammock with Kabāb on her chest. Resting a light hand on the newborn, she felt its irregular strained breathing. When the last lantern was snuffed out and the house was silent, she became aware of the sounds outside her window: the wind rustling through the bamboo, water flowing over stones, crickets chirping, and an occasional owl hooting.

Her mission was ending. The next day, when she was alone with Great-Aunt, she would relay the message to instigate insurgency from overseas. Once delivered, her assignment would be complete.

A quiet call came from outside. Was it a child or an animal? A response came back, just as quiet. The whispers rose to a crescendo, a sudden burst of animal-like sounds, followed by a play of back-and-forth from different directions.

She then heard a fragment of a song she had taught the children earlier and knew they were outside. The interplay between a tune she had learned growing up in America and the children's night calls warmed her. She tightened her embrace around Kabāb, whose breathing had become effortless, like a leaf cradled in the evening breeze before falling on the stillness of the earth.

When Maia woke the next morning, Kabāb was sound asleep. Great-Aunt and the children had gone off to the field. With Kabāb tied on her back, she followed the footpath through the bamboo where the children had emerged the day before. Beyond the thicket was expansive rolling red dirt, barren of all trees but overgrown with weeds.

Great-Aunt was assigning each child a strip of field along the hill's contours. Besides the children, several townspeople came to help.

"If the land were flat," a young man from town explained, "we could bulldoze the light brush and grasses. But it's uneven. We weed by hand." Thin and pale, he was a few years older than Maia. His accent told her that he was from a northern city.

Maia was given a strip between the man and Binh, who gladly reclaimed Kabāb.

"After the land is cleared and the soil tilled," the man told the children, "we'll sow the seeds two-by-two meters apart."

"We're planting a forest," Binh whispered, humming a lullaby to Kabāb.

The man dug at a spot near Maia. His voice lowered. "That's what this country needs—a new beginning. We can't wait for the old guards to die out. War poisoned their blood, and they're killing the country and people. We need to slash and burn to rid the poison. We can't do it alone. We need outside help."

The ground heated up and cracked under the sun. Great-Aunt, carrying a pouch of acacia seeds, moved easily among the children and townspeople. She stopped between Maia and the man. "I see you've met the children's teacher," she said, resting her gaze on Maia. "An intelligent man from public security. You must consider what he says."

The man locked eyes with Great-Aunt before setting off to help a child weed.

"You didn't imagine that you'd be doing this kind of fieldwork, did you?" Great-Aunt gave Maia eight glossy brown seeds and then got on her haunches and began pulling up the weeds around her. "Unlike Teacher, you look like you've done physical labor. It hardens the body and clears the mind."

Great-Aunt was right. Maia had spent many summers picking fruits and berries on New Jersey farms. This was her first time planting trees. Clearing and preparing the earth to sow the seeds, she felt at home among the children. She was reminded of her childhood working in the fields in America for her keep. She thought of her mother working the land while imprisoned.

She felt happy in sadness, connected in aloneness.

In the stillness of noon, hands and knees in the dirt, she decided not to pass on the message from overseas.

She slept that night with Kabāb on her chest. She dreamed of the children chanting and dancing in circles: arms raised, faces uplifted to the sky. Rain came. The acacia seeds sprouted, and the seedlings grew into trees. A forest was reborn.

Before daybreak, a slow sputter woke Maia. As soon as she became aware of the lightness on her chest, she knew Kabāb was not with her. She sprung from the hammock. Shadows flitted across the window. She dashed outside and saw the children trotting after the wooden boat pulled by the motorcycle-cartman. Binh ran haltingly with Kabāb bundled in his arms.

She trailed them on the footpath through the bamboo. They cut across the rolling fields they had cleared the day before. They entered a pine forest that grew along the mountainside. As they climbed, the sputter became faint, then fainter, then silent.

They reached the lake atop the mountain.

The cartman had unhitched the boat from his motorcycle, and the motley travelers were pushing the boat into the water.

The children rushed to the shore. Binh held the bundle out to Old Seeker.

Maia followed. "What are you doing?"

"Sixth Kabāb will go with them."

"Why?"

"To see the world!"

"What about home, father and mother?"

"No one will miss a piece of meat."

The children nodded.

Dawn came as gently as a cat's paw, nudging a sleeper awake.

"Everywhere is home," a child recited softly.

The children responded in unison, "Everyone is family."[19]

Binh continued to cradle the empty space in his arms after Old Seeker took Kabāb. "Don't make it cry," the boy said, and the child cried, as they had never heard it cry. Tears dropped into the lake. The children watched as the boat set off across the water that reflected a waning moon above and an orange sunrise in the horizon.

The Sea Lake

MORNING LIGHT PASSED through pine trees and refracted in still water. Maia and the children remained at the shore long after the boat was a speck on the horizon.

"Where do you think they're sailing to?" Maia asked the children.

"To the sea."

"The sea?"

"The lake has no bottom, linking it to the sea."

"It's our longing for the sea."

"It's salty, full of tears of the living for the dead."

Maia absorbed the children's stories. Retold from old tales or newly made-up, each tried to illuminate what *is*. She glimpsed their connectedness: what was visible on the children, she carried a sliver of within. She noticed the deformities less and less and recognized the children by their words and actions. Though distinct, they moved interdependently as if they were a part of a single mammoth being. She wondered whether they could continue in this human-created hell—living in isolation on the ranch, operating with the disfigurement handed to them.

Or could they find a way to transcend the illusory world of borders?

It was a Sunday, so the children had to fend for themselves. They swam and bathed in the lake and then scrubbed their scanty clothes on the flat boulders. They caught fish with bamboo poles and trawled for shrimps and crabs with wicker nets. They dug sweet cassavas from the ground and picked wild red berries off vines. They gathered dried leaves and twigs to start a fire. By midday, they had a feast that for a time filled the emptiness Kabāb's departure had left.

When evening came and a bright moon appeared, it was time for the children to return to the communal home. Maia stayed behind. The children headed off in a single file along the lake toward the pine forest. They moved with a lighthearted romping, as if dancing, singing the song they had just learned. The children disappeared into the forest, but she could still hear their voices. Alone by the lake, she joined in the dance.

> *Buffalo gals, won't you come out tonight,*
> *Come out tonight, come out tonight,*
> *Buffalo gals, won't you come out tonight,*
> *And dance by the light of the moon?*[20]

Night Calls

A COLD MIST came with nightfall and veiled the waning gibbous moon. Shadows flitted among the silent pines. When the air was still, Maia smelled a heavy odor of blood and decay. Two figures approached from afar. They stopped, leaning into one another, as if conversing. They parted, one retreating through the forest, the other coming toward her, empty-handed but carrying the nauseating smell of the midnight shuttle.

"The children told me you might be here," JP said, enfolding her into his arms.

"Uh, you need a bath."

"Aren't you curious where I've been?" He took off his bloodstained *L'amant* T-shirt and khaki pants.

"You should wash your clothes, too."

He was now naked. "Is this the lake of your father's letter?" He stepped into the dark glassy water and submerged himself. He vanished and then surfaced, floating easily on his back.

"It's warm and salty and buoyant," he said, "like the sea."

Water undulated, ripples spreading across stillness.

"Come, Maia!"

And she did.

They swam in the lake, cold air above and warm water below. The buoyancy lifted them, and they let go to the embrace. Two bodies moved as one. The mist swirled like a dance of white cloth above. The water cupped them below.

When their skin cooled, though inside remained hot, they left the lake and lay on a flat boulder.

"Do you remember the soldier we picked up on the shuttle?" JP asked.

"I can't forget his smell."

"He's coming back in the morning to take me across the border to where the locals have sighted a group of men. One of them could be my brother."

"Can you trust him?"

"It's my only lead."

"I'm not coming to translate for you if that's why you're here."

"I'm not looking for a translator."

Night calls burst from silence, startling JP, and he reached for her hand.

"It's the children," she said.

Lying side by side, they listened to the back-and-forth calls that encircled them in a rawness of flowing emotions. She could identify many of the voices as belonging to the children, but two did not: clear resounding voices she could not pin down but had heard from the previous nights. She was reminded of the odd duet on Waiting Mountain when their animal-like calls transformed the bare peak into a lush forest. An inexplicable lightness filled her. The mist thinned and unveiled the moon above and its reflection below in the pearl-shaped lake. Turning to JP in the silvery light, she whispered *yes* to the question he had not asked. *Yes.*

Uprising

THEY WOKE TO an uprising.

The morning sky was black with smoke. Red flames rose from the direction of town. Without a word, Maia dashed from the lakeside to the pines. JP followed.

Several treetops caught fire from flying embers. Maia and JP cut through the forest, crossing the open field of planted acacia seeds and entering the bamboo thicket. Through the screen of bamboo, they saw the longhouse engulfed in flame. All around, tussocks blazed like bonfires. Spreading quickly, the fire consumed the young bamboo grove.

They hid behind the stone well. Shielded from the intense heat, they watched for movement and listened for voices inside Great-Aunt's home. Except for thatch crackling and a sweet putrid odor of burning flesh, there was nothing more.

In the distance, they heard screams from all directions.

After the longhouse was in smoldering ruins, uniformed men from public security arrived. They covered their noses with white handkerchiefs and rambled about. They kicked at what seemed like a charred tree trunk amidst the rubble. When there was no movement, the men left.

"Who are they looking for?" JP whispered.

She slouched against the well, squeezing into a tight ball to still herself.

The wind picked up the remains of the home. Ashes swirled in the sky.

Maia and JP did not notice the soldier from the shuttle until he stood beside them. The smoke masked his stench. He told them three major towns on the Central Highlands had held peaceful demonstrations. The events had turned violent when public security rounded up the leaders and dispersed the protesters. The government had declared a freeze on all movement on the highlands. No entering or exiting.

The fog came at dusk. Whispers seeped out from the darkness. People were on the move again.

A call. A response. Singing.

Children sang in harmony, echoing a duet's lead.

The soldier tracked the night calls. "That's the way," he finally said and beckoned.

JP shadowed him into the fog.

Maia rose in the mist that was a dance of obscurity and revelation. The fire burned, but the warmth she felt was from knowing the children were making their way westward. She turned east and followed the pass from the mountain to the sea.

Epilogue

CURTAINS LIKE WHITE cumulus clouds billowed through windows. Laughter mingled with the wind rustling through the holes in thatched walls. PHOENIX SALON, a faded sign hung on the door. The beauty shop on the outskirts of the highlands appeared dilapidated, but Maia wanted to wash the burnt odor from her hair. When she lifted the wooden latch, the door swung open and she felt a cold breeze. The curtains flapped and the roof fluttered as if they wanted to fly. A sweet scent of ripe guava filled the airy salon. She smelled something else. Only here it was not subdued but pulsating, sucking her in.

"Close the door," a voice called. "You're from across the bridge?"

"She's not from across the bridge," a second voice said. "Can't you tell? She's from down south."

"My family moved to Saigon during the summer of red fire."

"The girl now lives in America," a third voice said.

"Come, over here!"

All the chairs were taken, except one.

"Be careful," the woman with a stylish bob warned. "Go around." She pointed to the mossy craters in the floor, brimming with water.

Maia stepped around the basins toward the empty seat where a woman was sweeping with a straw broom. The woman did not look up but continued to make scratching sounds on the ground. Her long side-swept bangs hid part of her face.

"No. No. Not there." The woman with the bob stood up and motioned Maia into the now vacant seat. "I'm the hairstylist." She pointed to the sweeper and whispered, "Don't be afraid. That's the salon owner. And the ponytail over there is the beautician. She can pluck your eyebrows, give you a facial, and make you honeysome."

"You should only be afraid of ma sống," someone said.

There were fewer customers than she had thought. The voices and laughter seemed fainter now, as if coming from outside, in the walls, or beneath the ground.

"I just want a shampoo."

The hairstylist slipped off Maia's sandals and placed her feet into a bowl of cool soothing water. Bony fingers massaged her soles in slow circular motions.

As she eased into the chair, a sigh released from somewhere pent-up. She tilted her head into a basin and gazed at the afternoon sky through a large hole in the ceiling. What could have fallen through the roof, breaking up the earth—a hand grenade, a rock from a meteor storm falling like fire, a ball thrown from the past in an arc to a future catcher? The hole might have been smaller, but the monsoons had enlarged the sphere, morphing its roundness into an amorphous, gaping sky.

Water sluiced over her head, and fingers kneaded her scalp, lathering up suds that smelled sweet and tart. Closing her eyes, she saw light twirling. The sky pulsated to a slow beat of a tune at the edge of memory, like a ballad she had heard ferrying across a river in late afternoon.

"Is the girl here?" A briny smell of the sea drifted into the salon.

The scraping of the broom on the floor stopped.

"Come in. Close the door."

"Oh, heaven-earth. The girl's so dark. Just like when she was born. Dark like a child of a black GI."

When you were born, your skin was so dark and hair so frizzy your aunt complained to the hospital about a mix-up. Back then the Americans were still here.

"Not a bit of your father." A perceptible sigh enveloped the room.

Maia held her breath. She was again eavesdropping in the house of her childhood.

"You're here to gawk or shampoo and blow dry?"

"Can you make it quick?"

The chair squeaked beside her.

"I haven't got to the market yet. Sweet-sour fish soup, steamed anchovy loaf, boiled greens."

The sound of running water muffled the voices.

"The girl still speaks her mother tongue, doesn't she? I'd learn English, but this head of mine and all those *to be* verbs: *I am. You are. We are. They are. He, she, it is.* Oh, heaven-earth! What use is *to be* now?"

The water stopped.

"Roller set or blow dry?"

"Just blow dry, some waves and curls."

The hum of a hair dryer filled the room.

"It was my fate, the nun at Ox Pagoda predicted. I accept. But hers? Is she asleep?"

Light twirled through the hole in the roof and the sky pressed on her closed eyelids. "Why did you believe in prophecy?" *she wanted to ask, but her head was spinning, her tongue heavy. What were the words she copied in neat cursive on the inside cover of her high school journal? Something about chance. Something about choice. What's destiny in Vietnam-ese? What's Vietnamese for chance? For choice?*

"She wanted a shampoo and then fell asleep. She must have been in the fire. Her hair smells of smoke."

We waited, Ba and I, in the Eastern Sea. In my dream, I saw you swimming in Grandma's garden from the second-floor balcony. Up and down rows and rows of miniature yellow roses, purple dragon fruit, and mai bonsai you swam. Freestyle, backstroke, then butterfly. By the starfruit tree you treaded water, watching a school of angelfish glide by. The fish had escaped from Uncle's pond. In Ba's dream, you'd fallen into the well under the guava tree, but he couldn't bail you out. It was a dream—a nightmare. Wasn't it?

"Okay, beautiful as always." The hair dryer stopped. "What kind of fish soup? Butterfish, sea bass, catfish?"

"Whatever One-Eye has caught."

A gust of wind blew the door open, and the smell of the ocean faded.

Murmured voices and occasional laughter mingled with the monotonous scratching of the broom on the floor.

"You're awake." Fingers kneaded her scalp.

Through the hole in the roof, she could see the gray after-noon sky. Rainclouds cast shadows into the salon.

"What about a haircut?" the stylist asked, untangling her long damp hair with a wide-tooth comb.

In the mirror Maia caught sight of the sweeper. The woman looked up. Her side-swept bangs fell back and re-vealed a scar on her forehead.

"You should layer your hair," the woman said. "It softens your cheekbones."

Something made Maia agree. When she met the woman's gaze in the mirror again, she knew hers was one of the voices she had heard earlier.

The stylist cut her hair with an easy flowing motion. When done, she asked, "What do you think?"

Her straight long hair, now blunt cut, had layered sides, feather-like. Looking at herself in the mirror, she felt different. She grasped the warm ball that swelled in her. When she stood up to leave, the room seemed to spin, and its walls dissolved, making her dizzy as if she were standing in the riverbed of a world in flux. She edged toward the door. The craters in the ground seemed cavernous, dark and vast.

"Wait!" the woman with long side-swept bangs called. "Take this." She handed her a faded red basket.

"That's not mine."

"It's your mother's," she said. "Follow the stream. Go across the bridge to the marketplace. You can't miss her."

The watercourse meandered along the edge of the forest. She looped the straps of the shopping basket around her shoulder. The plastic, once sturdy and red, was now lucent pink. She would fit right in, sauntering to the market in the yellow đồ bộ. But she was walking too fast, almost running, kicking up dust and pebbles that trapped between her sandals and feet.

The stream entered the woods, leaves rustled, and birds chirped. They sounded celebratory. She did not accelerate into a sprint as she did on the cross-country trails she had run in high school—*Nike Air* sneakers, spandex tights under yellow-and-white school uniform when the autumn air turned cold in the Northeast, head full of imaginings of the future. The trail was always a loop, circling back to the starting line, to bystanders' cheers and the final push. Now entering the forest, she slowed to a walk. Her hair was drenched with sweat. She was hungry and her mouth salivated, remembering the tart and sweet fragrance of a ripened fruit. She stopped to splash cool water onto her face and took a big gulp.

She heard voices. When she looked up, she saw moving shadows. Some were bobbing in the water. *Follow the stream,* they had said. *Go across the bridge to the marketplace.* She had left the salon and walked downstream. Should she have gone the other way? That would have led her back to town and she did not remember a bridge.

The forest seemed young, no ancient banyans rooting into the earth, no lofty redwoods reaching for the sky. The trees were lean and lush, too sparse to shade the pockmarked ground. Here and there, the watercourse widened into shallow basins. In one of these craters, she came upon a group of women on their haunches, washing clothes, sifting rice, and cleaning vegetables. Some were bathing, long black hair coursing down naked backs.

"Why so late?" a woman asked, floating in midstream. Her central lowlands accent had a northern air. "You'd better hurry. The fish are fresh today."

"Could you tell me where the market is?"

"You're not from around here?" The woman looked at her closely. "That's right, you're the daughter. Why so small and dark?"

"Those Westerners," a naked woman interjected, wringing water from her hair and twisting it into a knot. "Tall like Noël trees, big like rice wine barrels, and white like daikon."

The women laughed. They appeared to be in their mid-forties, robust and mature, but bantered like a group of young girls.

"Bigmouth! That's why no men are around."

"Sister talks as if she had a man. With her lacquered black smile—"

"Go ahead, girl." The women laughed and waved their hands. "Follow the stream. Do you smell that? That's where the market is. That's Old Charcoal, roasting wild boar. Most delicious is the fatty, crispy skin, with jungle moonshine for fertility."

She left the women and followed the dirt path. From a distance, their voices rose and fell like frenzied creatures' mating calls. Where the stream emptied into a lake, she saw a footbridge swaying in the breeze. *Go across the bridge to the marketplace.* She looked around. She heard the buzzing of a market and smelled roasted meat. She crossed the footbridge.

The open marketplace spread along the lakeside.

"Mua đi! Mua đi!" a blind peddler cried, clutching her basket of pink mountain apples.

"Come buy! Come buy! Fresh fish. Sweet fruit. Roasted pig. Come try!"

The aroma of barbecue lured her toward an old woman tending a fire pit. She was fanning the flame as the carcass sizzled, dripping fat, and the smoke rose. When the woman looked up, her scorched black features startled Maia.

"Roasted pig?" asked the charred skull. "Jungle moonshine?"

Maia backed away and merged into the market.

Fish plopped in shallow water on silver trays. A shrimp leapt. Sea-green crabs crawled in box steps. Bright dragon fruit in pyramids, green guavas in woven baskets, spiny red rambutans in bunches, yellow jackfruits split open, fragrant and sweet. Leafy green vegetables, fresh herbs, pickled roots. Ground spices came from near and far. Anchovy. Fertilized duck eggs, thousand-year-old preserved eggs.

Maia saw a woman with shoulder-length hair. The woman walked with a light bounce, moving through the aisles. She reminded Maia of a farmer who balanced two baskets with a pole on his shoulders. *It's the bounce that keeps the heavy load off*, the farmer had said. The woman stopped here and there, haggled over the prices, paid, and then left without taking her purchases. She stopped at the fish vendor, then vegetables, then spices.

"Little miss! Little miss! Which do you like?" A fishmonger pointed to a tank full of fish when Maia passed by. He watched her from one eye, the other a dark hollow socket. "Which do you like? Choose one!"

In a swarm of silvery sea-green, a small flash of pink caught her eyes.

"Con cá hồng?" The one-eyed fishmonger saw her focus.

He swooped his net into the tank, a swirling commotion, and caught a willowy pink fish with glossy dark round eyes. He plopped it onto his wooden chopping block and raised his sharpened cleaver.

"No! Oh no! Can I have it alive?"

"Not clean? Scale? Gut?"

"Can you put it in a bag with some water?"

Lowering the cleaver, he picked up the fish by the tail, dropped it into a bag, and filled it halfway with water. He tied the bag with a rubber band and handed it to her. "It's paid for," he said and pointed her to the vegetable vendor, where she picked up tomatoes, pineapple chunks, okra, tamarinds, and fresh herbs for sweet-sour soup.

Maia followed the woman, stopping at the same vendors to collect more purchased items. She picked up pork belly and salted fish for steamed anchovy loaf and rau muống for boiling, then shallots, garlic, and chili peppers. The basket was getting full. Sweet-sour soup, mắm chưng, boiled greens. What was missing? Eggs. She remembered the rooster from before the sea crossing and the red hen on the other shore. She bargained with a fair-skinned girl and paid two thousand đồng for four eggs.

She looked around and saw the woman talking with the bird merchant. Birds of all varieties twittered in bamboo crates. The woman pointed to the swallows. They haggled and she paid. The peddler caught a brown pair and placed them in a small wicker carrier. With the birdcage dangling in one hand, the woman left the market, the wind ruffling her hair, the swallows chirping.

Maia followed the woman along the shore. They reached the river that drained the lake. An ancient stone bridge arched across the water like a still moon above shifting currents. The graceful circular lines created a sense of peace, though it was a passage of war, one that had served an army's movement. As she got closer, Maia saw that it had been seriously damaged, with jagged gaps that small vehicles could fall through.

When the woman neared the crossing, she released the birds from the cage. The pair fluttered hesitantly, a pink evening glow on their wings. The swallows swerved and floated and soared across the sky.

"Má!" Maia called out a single word that came to her.

The woman turned.

Maia gazed into her own face, only a few years older. "Má?"

They stepped together onto the bridge that arched across the river like a crescent moon. They walked around the holes and cracks, through which they could see the water rushing below. Across the river the land dipped and then rose, a rolling field of emptiness under the red evening sun. They came to a large jagged opening on the bridge.

"Be careful." The woman took her hand. "Jump!"

They leaped the gap. In the river, sky.

Notes

1. The legend of Bà Triệu is based on my reading about Triệu Thị Trinh in David G. Marr's *Vietnamese Tradition on Trial*, 1920–1945.

2. The poem is an abbreviated translation of Trạng Quỳnh's explanation of his five-fruit painting in the tale "Thi Ngũ Quả."

3. "The Party's Three Delays" is from David Chanoff and Doan Van Toai's *'Vietnam': A Portrait of its People at War.*

4. The idea of interbeing is from Thich Nhat Hanh's *Love in Action: Writings on Nonviolent Social Change.*

5. The lyrics are translated from Lê Thương's "Hòn Vọng Phu 3."

6. "Dewdrops" is by Nolan W. K. Kim.

7. The poem "Mới Ra Tù Tập Leo Núi" is a Vietnamese version of Hồ Chí Minh's poem written in Chinese after his release from prison in southern China in 1943. The poem appears in *Nhật Ký Trong Tù / Prison Diary.*

8. The lines are from Hồ Chí Minh's letter to the indigenous minorities in Pleiku.

9. The lyrics are translated from Nguyễn Văn Thương and Kim Minh's "Đêm Đông."

10. The idea of eternal return is from Friedrich Nietzsche's *Thus Spoke Zarathustra*, trans. Graham Parkes.

11. The passage is from *Zhuangzi*, trans. Hyun Höchsmann and Yang Guorong.

12. The passages are from *Sun-tzu: The Art of Warfare*, trans. Roger T. Ames.

13. The hymn to Mother Earch is based on my reading about Pô Nagar in Nguyễn Thế Anh's essay in *Essays into Vietnamese Pasts*, eds. K.W. Taylor and John K. Whitmore.

14. The quote is by William Jennings Bryan.

15. The rumor that Hòn Vọng Phu had crumbled and scattered in the ocean is mentioned in Andrew Lam's "The Stories They Carried" in *Perfume Dreams: Reflections on the Vietnamese Diaspora*.

16. The quote is from Dale Carnegie's *How to Stop Worrying and Start Living*.

17. The lyrics are translated from Lê Thương's "Hòn Vọng Phu 1."

18. The lyrics are translated from Lê Thương's "Hòn Vọng Phu 2."

19. The lines spoken by the children are adapted from Subramanian Shankar's translation of Kanian Poongundranar's "yaadhum oore, yaavarum kelir."

20. The lyrics (from John Hodges' 1844 "Buffalo Gals," originally published as "Lubly Fan") are quoted from Ursula K. Le Guin's "Buffalo Gals, Won't You Come Out Tonight."

Acknowledgments

Fire Summer is a work of fiction. While many characters are inspired by real life, places depicted have geographical correspondence, and events are noted in history, the story is fictitious. I am grateful to the John Young Scholarship in the Arts for enabling my research in Vietnam in 2007. I thank my dissertation committee at the University of Hawai'i at Mānoa: Craig Howes for my essential gesture, Cristina Bacchilega for asking questions of stones, and Robert Onopa for saying *no* in 1965 and *yes* in 2010. I am indebted to my teachers—Colleen Majors at Stephen Girard Elementary School; Ed Kiernan, Joan Gucken, Nancy Tregnan, and especially Naomi Kuziemski for her loving guidance at the Philadelphia High School for Girls; John O'Neill, Douglas Raybeck, and William Rosenfeld at Hamilton College; Paul Lyons, Kathy Phillips, Mark Heberle, Reinhard Friederich, Robert Shapard, Ian MacMillan, Steven Goldsberry, and Chung-ying Cheng at the University of Hawai'i at Mānoa. I thank Frank Gallo, Susan Branz, Cuong Mai, Kazuyo Karan, Jacinta Suataute Galea'i, Jocelyn Cardenas, Ralph Lalepa Koga, Michael and Tiffany Tsai, Bruce and Mahany Lindquist, and Mark McGrath and Janet J. Graham for friendship; Kate Gale, Mark E. Cull, Tobi Harper, Monica Fernandez, Natasha McClellan, Rebeccah Sanhueza, and Tansica Sunkamaneevongse at the impeccable Red Hen Press for shepherding a hatchling; Jennifer Lyons for literary representation and much more; Nolan W. K. Kim, Gypsy Love-Sponge, Bingo Hunkaluv, Moñino Crawdad, Sophie Charlotte Mucho Más, and Matilda Lani Abdullah for love, inspiration, and the journey home.

Biographical Note

Thuy Da Lam was born in Qui Nhơn, grew up in Philadelphia, and now lives in Honolulu, where she works on her next book and teaches at Kapiʻolani Community College.

She holds a BA in creative writing from Hamilton College and a PhD in English from the University of Hawaiʻi at Mānoa. She received the George A. Watrous Literary Prize for Fiction, the Myrle Clark Writing Award, and the John Young Scholarship in the Arts. *Fire Summer* is a revision of her dissertation, part of which appeared in *Lost Lake Folk Opera* in commemoration of the fortieth anniversary of the end of the Vietnam War.